FOCUS ON THE FAMILY®

Christian Heritage Series

THE CHARLESTON YEARS

The Escape

Nancy Rue

BETHANY HOUSE PUBLISHERS
MINNEAPOLIS, MINNESOTA 55438

This author is represented by the literary agency of Alive Communications, 1465 Kelly Johnson Blvd., Suite 320, Colorado Springs, CO 80920.

This story is a work of fiction. All characters are the product of the author's imagination. Any resemblance to any person, living or dead, is coincidental.

A Focus on the Family book
Published by Bethany House Publishers
A Ministry of Bethany Fellowship International
11400 Hampshire Avenue South
Minneapolis, Minnesota 55438
www.bethanyhouse.com

Printed in the United States of America by
Bethany Press International, Minneapolis, Minnesota 55438

Library of Congress Cataloging-in-Publication Data

Rue, Nancy N.
    The escape / Nancy Rue.
        p.   cm. — (The Christian heritage series, the Charleston years ;
bk. 6)
    Summary: As fighting erupts between the North and the South, eleven-year-old Austin helps his slave friend gain freedom before making his own escape from Charleston, South Carolina.
    ISBN 1–56179–639–5
    [1. Escapes—Fiction. 2. Slavery—Fiction. 3. Charleston (S.C.)—History—Fiction. 4. Christian life—Fiction.] I. Title. II. Series: Rue, Nancy N. Christian heritage series, the Charleston Years ; bk. 6.
PZ7.R88515Es   1998
[Fic]—dc21   98–25554
                                                                              CIP
                                                                               AC

99 00 01 02 03 04 05 /15 14 13 12 11 10 9 8 7 6 5 4 3 2

For all who have braved the storms

for freedom and equality

A Map of
Charleston
1860-1861

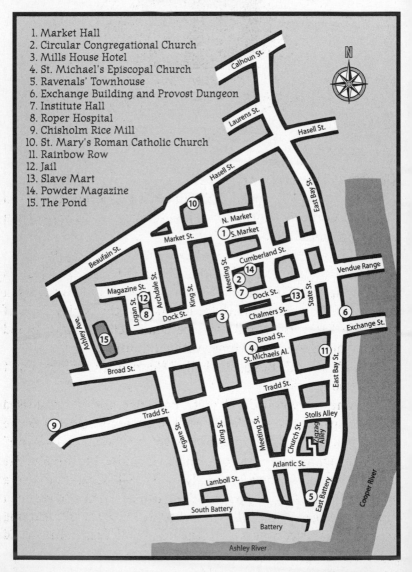

1. Market Hall
2. Circular Congregational Church
3. Mills House Hotel
4. St. Michael's Episcopal Church
5. Ravenals' Townhouse
6. Exchange Building and Provost Dungeon
7. Institute Hall
8. Roper Hospital
9. Chisholm Rice Mill
10. St. Mary's Roman Catholic Church
11. Rainbow Row
12. Jail
13. Slave Mart
14. Powder Magazine
15. The Pond

Chapter One

"Call it out, Henry-James!"

As she spoke, Polly Ravenal tossed her head—on purpose, Austin knew, just to make the thick ostrich feather on her felt hat dance.

"Call it out!" she said again. "Call out, 'Ready, set, go'!"

But on the ground below them, Henry-James crinkled his forehead up at the two horses. From where Austin Hutchinson sat, behind his cousin Charlotte Ravenal on the back of one of his Uncle Drayton's blood bays, he could tell his slave friend wasn't about to obey *that* order without a fuss.

"I don't like this none, Miz Polly," Henry-James said. "I don't like this none a'tall."

"No one said you had to like it," Polly said primly. She tossed her head again. "I'm sure Tot doesn't like everything I tell her to do, but you don't see her questioning her mistress, now do you?"

Austin could feel Charlotte snorting under her breath. He looked down at stumpy Tot, Polly's personal slave, and gave a snort of his own. The way poor Tot's mouth constantly hung open and her eyes gaped, she *always* looked like she was questioning something as far as he was concerned. But Polly was right—she'd

1

never argue with her mistress, even if Polly told her to jump in a well or climb up a chimney.

Not like Henry-James, Austin thought as he watched him cross his arms over his chest and continue squinting up at Polly. Most of the time he liked Henry-James that way—smart and brave and as independent as a slave could get.

But at times like this, when he, Charlotte, Polly, and his little brother, Jefferson, wanted to just hurtle headlong into an adventure, it would be nice if Henry-James wouldn't *think* so much.

From his position behind Polly on the bay mare, seven-year-old Jefferson Hutchinson wriggled so he could look around Polly. "Come on, Henry-James!" he whined. "We want to race!"

"I knows you does," Henry-James said. "And I ain't about to 'low it till I knows you all is gonna be safe."

Polly sat up straight in the saddle and tugged at her fitted red riding jacket. "What did I hear, Henry-James?" she said. "Did I hear you say you weren't going to 'allow it'?"

"Yes'm," Henry-James said. "That's 'zactly what I done said."

Polly looked at Charlotte and Austin with her hand spread across the frill at her throat.

"Where on earth do you think he got the idea that he—a *slave*—can *allow* or *not* allow *me*—his mistress—to do anything?"

" 'Scuse me, Miz Polly," Henry-James said, "but I's Marse Drayton's slave first, and he done tol' me if'n anything ever happen to you chilrun whilst I's lookin' after you, he gonna put me right in his pocket."

At that, Henry-James's bloodhound-mutt, Bogie, lifted his baggy-skinned head from his nap spot on the ground beside Henry-James and blinked fiercely.

"Nothing's going to happen to us, Henry-James," Charlotte said quickly.

Charlotte wasn't one for flapping her lips a lot—not like

Austin himself. But Austin knew she was as aware as he was—and even Bogie was—what "put me right in his pocket" meant. Those words were worse than a whipping. They meant the master was going to sell his slave away from everyone and everything he knew.

"You can't say that for certain, Miz Lottie," Henry-James said. "You all's about to race these here horses—and as I sees it, jus' about *anything* could happen."

"Pooh!" Polly said. She gave the neat little riding jacket another indignant tug. "Both Charlotte and I are excellent riders, and my father has been working with Jefferson the entire time he's been here. How long has that been—over a year?" She rolled her eyes. "He can at least hang on by now!"

"I could do more than that!" Jefferson wailed. Austin groaned as he watched Jefferson's chubby cheeks go scarlet and the sweat start to bead at the roots of his curvy black hair. "I could ride this horse all by my own self! I don't even need Polly on here with me! I ride better than Austin! He couldn't ride *his* own horse!"

"Hush up, shrimp!" Austin said.

"Come on, Henry-James," Charlotte said. "Just call it out. I promise you no one's going to get hurt."

Once again Henry-James looked at them with his forehead wrinkled and his eyes in slits. His arms with their bigger-than-the-usual–13-year-old's muscles slid from their crossed position down to his hips, and he stood there surveying the four of them. Polly sighed impatiently and pulled yet again at her jacket and examined the dust on the matching red boots and smoothed out her plaid underskirt. But she didn't say a word. They all knew to wait until Henry-James had thought it all the way through and was sure about his decision. Even Bogie seemed to be holding his breath.

Austin fidgeted. He wanted to race now more than ever. He was stinging from his little brother's remark. And not just the remark, but the fact that it was true.

"All right, then," Henry-James said finally. "You all ready? You got you a good seat on them saddles?"

Polly sniffed for her answer. Charlotte nodded and gripped the reins. Austin slid his arms around her middle and hung on.

"Massa Jefferson?" Henry-James said.

"I don't have to hold on!" Jefferson cried.

"Then there ain't gonna be no race."

"Don't be such a child, Jefferson," Polly said.

"He *is* a child," Austin whispered to Charlotte.

But his words were lost in a series of shouts from Henry-James.

"Ready! Set! You all—go!"

Henry-James let his arm drop, and Bogie threw back his big head and howled. Austin felt the blood bay leap forward almost before Charlotte punched her heels into his sides. She slanted forward over the horse's neck, and Austin slanted with her.

Right away the scene around them became a blur. All the colors of a South Carolina spring—chinaberry trees with their hundreds of flowers and the azaleas with their thick clumps of blossoms—smeared past them as Charlotte and Austin flew down the buggy road, the horse kicking up dust, Charlotte bouncing her boots against his ribs, and Austin doing all he could do—which was cling to Charlotte until he thought he'd squeeze her in two.

And, of course, talk.

"We're way ahead of them, Lottie!" he called into her ear. "You must be going nine miles an hour—maybe even 10! They're having our dust for dinner!"

That was true, but only for a moment. Austin had no more than spoken when the mare's hoofbeats thundered louder from behind them and he could hear Jefferson squealing.

"Faster!" Austin cried.

Charlotte nodded and leaned all the way down to the horse's

ear. Austin leaned with her and thought he was going to fold in half. He lifted his face to look ahead of them. An idea immediately sprang up.

"Jump the hedge!" he shouted to Charlotte. "Polly will never try it!"

He could almost feel Charlotte grinning. Not only did they look enough alike to be 12-year-old twins instead of cousins, with their identical deer-colored hair and their freckled, turned-up Ravenal noses and their amber-brown eyes, but they also thought alike. All Austin had to do was suggest something, and Charlotte was halfway there.

Laughing into the still-crisp March air, she lifted the horse lightly over the boxwood hedge, cutting out the curve in the buggy road. Austin chanced a glance over his shoulder.

Just as he'd predicted, Polly hadn't taken the hedge. She was galloping madly around the curve. Jefferson was holding on with only one hand. The other was waving in a fist over his head at Austin.

"Ha *ha*!" Austin shouted at him.

The little fist shook. Austin turned loose of Charlotte just for an instant to shake his in return.

"Hang on, Austin!" Charlotte cried. "We're taking the next hedge!"

Austin flailed to get his arm back around Charlotte—just as the horse left the ground. Caught by surprise, Austin swayed crazily to the right.

"Hang on!" Charlotte cried again.

But she couldn't slow down now—not in midair. The horse sailed on, and so did Austin, but in a different direction. The ground spun dizzily as it came up to meet him. Every limb hit it at a different moment—elbow then knee then foot then shoulder. Even to himself he sounded like a bag of apples emptying onto the dirt.

Austin scrambled up before the last joint made contact, his mouth going faster than Charlotte's horse.

"You're winning, Lottie! She'll never catch you—keep going!"

Whether she heard him or not, he was never sure. It didn't seem to matter. The minute she cleared the hedge back to the buggy road, Charlotte reined in the horse and came down from his back in a flurry of petticoats and pantelettes.

Even as Polly and Jefferson flew past her, Polly was shouting, "Charlotte Ravenal—act like a lady!"

Charlotte did nothing of the kind as she leapfrogged over the hedge and tore toward Austin.

"You let them win!" Austin cried.

"Are you hurt?"

"Of course not! Why did you stop? You were way ahead of them!"

By then Polly and Jefferson had passed the finish line—the row of crepe myrtles—and were shouting their victory. Someone else was shouting, too. Henry-James jumped over the first hedge with Bogie on his heels and hurled himself at Austin.

"I knowed I shouldn'ta let you race! I knowed it!"

"You have to let us race again!" Austin said. His elbows were starting to sting, but he forced himself not to clutch at them. "I messed it all up when I fell off!"

"You certainly did!" Polly called from atop her triumphant horse. She looked back over her shoulder at Jefferson. "It's really too bad, isn't it?"

Jefferson grinned his dimples into place. "Sure is!"

"No!" Austin said. "We have to start over or it won't be a fair race!"

"I don't care about no fair race," Henry-James said. "You lucky you wasn't killed, Massa Austin!"

"I wasn't even close to being killed," Austin said. By now his knees were smarting, too, but he wouldn't have admitted it if they'd been shattered like eggshells.

"Uh huh," Henry-James said. "You got you a big ol' raspberry on the side of your face."

Austin touched his left cheek and tried not to wince. Then he sneaked a look at his bloody fingers as Henry-James turned to Polly and Jefferson.

"I reckon you done won—and now it be over," Henry-James said.

Jefferson waved his hands wildly over his head, and Polly gave a satisfied sniff.

"Don't look so proud of your sweet selves," Austin said. "You only won because I fell off."

"We still would have won," Polly said. "You two cheated."

Jefferson's face brightened. "Yeah! You cheated!"

"We did not either!" Charlotte burst out.

She stomped to the hedge and glared up at Polly, who slid off her horse without revealing so much as an inch of lace and stood with her hands folded at her waist.

"You most certainly did," she said. "No one said you could jump the hedge."

"No one said we couldn't!"

Austin was sure it was going to turn into one of Polly and Charlotte's nose-tweaking, hair-pulling sessions. And it might have if Tot hadn't huffed and puffed her way around the curve, sweat glistening on her kinky-haired head. She hauled her stubby self between the two girls and stood there, mouth gaping at Charlotte.

Austin had to smirk. The closest Tot ever came to standing up to anyone was when she was defending Polly. What she would have done if Charlotte had shoved her out of the way, nobody knew. It was enough just to see her standing there.

"I don't see how it makes no difference a'tall," said Henry-James. "It wasn't nothin' but a game. It don't mean nothin'." He turned and narrowed his eyes at Austin. "What do matter is Massa Austin standin' there bleedin' like that. You best let me look at them wounds."

He took a step toward Austin, shaking his head the way Austin's *mother* used to do when he was Jefferson's age. It made his shoulder blades pinch together.

"I don't need to be looked at," he said. "I'm fine."

"You don't look fine," Polly chimed in.

"I ought to know whether I'm fine or not," Austin said. He could feel his face getting hot. "And I'm *fine*!"

"Maybe you should let him just check," Charlotte said in a tiny voice.

"No. I'm not hurt. All I did was come off a horse."

"You *fell* off, you mean," Jefferson said.

"You hush up, shrimp!"

"Come on, Massa Austin, don't give me no trouble," Henry-James said. "I's re-*spon*-sible for you."

Before Austin could tell him *again* that he didn't need tending to, Henry-James reached out and curled his fingers around Austin's wrist. Although Austin tugged hard, he couldn't get loose.

"Let go!" he said.

"Now, Massa—"

"Let *go*!" Austin tried again to jerk his hand away. When Henry-James's fingers stayed solid as iron bands, Austin kicked out his foot and caught the slave boy behind the knee. For an instant, Henry-James's leg gave, and Austin gave him a shove with his other hand to push him off balance. He found himself flat on his back on the ground, with Henry-James straddling him.

✢✦✢

Chapter Two

Henry-James looked down at him, smiling enough to reveal the wide gap between his two front teeth.

"Now what was you tryin' to do there, Massa Austin?" he said.

"I'm wrestling you!" Austin said. "Somebody's got to show you that I'm perfectly fine!"

"You may be, Boston," Polly said, her voice going into a cackle. "But you'll never wrestle Henry-James!"

Henry-James pulled himself off Austin and put a hand down to help him up. Austin pushed it away and stood. Both elbows, both knees, his left cheek, and the heel of his left hand were all sizzling with scrapes. He glowered at Polly.

"And why not?" he said.

"Because," she said. She cocked her plumed hat at him, as if she were surprised he'd even asked. "It's such a . . . well, such a masculine thing, wrestling is. That isn't your style, Boston. You're more . . . bookish."

She nodded at Tot, who, of course, bobbed her head eagerly in return. Jefferson, too, nodded.

"That's just the way you are, Austin," Charlotte said, her voice in a hurry. "There's nothing wrong with it. We like you that way."

"Ain't no need to even talk about it," Henry-James said. He turned his face slightly away from Austin.

There was a strange silence—an odd one for their little group. It was as if no one knew what to say next, and that *never* happened. A voice calling timidly from the direction of the Big House filled in the uncomfortable space.

"Miz Polly! Miz Polly! Missus want you right quick!"

It was Mousie, Aunt Olivia's personal slave woman. The only time she spoke was to deliver messages for her mistress. The rest of the time she scampered around silently behind Aunt Olivia, carrying a basket of plantation keys that was bigger than she was. Of course, *most* things were bigger than she was.

"Whatever does Mama want *now*?" Polly said.

Tot shrugged. Austin didn't even wonder. His head was still spinning with what he'd just heard.

"Masculine. That isn't your style, Boston. You're more . . . bookish."

Austin sneaked a pat at one of his hurting elbows. *I am bookish*, he thought. *And Charlotte's right—there's nothing wrong with that. I learned that when we first came here to Canaan Grove.*

Then why did it suddenly hurt so much to hear it said?

"Polly!" called out another voice.

This time it was Uncle Drayton, slowing his black gelding to a halt just beyond the hedge, his frock coat settling down behind him, his brown brocade waistcoat shining in the sun. Everyone stiffened just a little—except Tot and Henry-James, who stiffened a lot.

"Don't you hear your mother callin' you?" he said. His voice, though always smooth as southern honey, held a touch of impatience. It kept anybody from pointing out that it was actually Mousie who was calling.

"I'm going, Daddy," Polly said with a pout. "Here, Henry-James, you take the horse back to the stables."

Uncle Drayton straightened his tall, thin frame in his saddle and drilled his Ravenal eyes into Henry-James from under his wide-brimmed hat.

"You haven't been ridin' the horses, have you, boy?" he said.

Henry-James lowered his eyes. "No, sir," he said. "I wouldn't do none of that, Marse Drayton. I knows I ain't 'lowed to."

That was one item on the arm-long list of things slaves weren't allowed to do, according to the Slave Code. Uncle Drayton was strict about all his "property" sticking to it.

Now he took his eyes off Henry-James and swept them back to Polly. They grew a little softer, and he smiled at her.

He had such a manly roughness woven into the expensive suit and the neatly trimmed beard and the elegant way he had of sitting. It clicked in Austin's mind like snapping fingers.

That was what had so impressed him the first day he'd met Uncle Drayton, when his own father had brought him and his mother, Sally Hutchinson, and Jefferson to Canaan Grove to stay with Mother's brother while he went on to travel as an abolitionist lecturing against slavery. His mother was too sick to live that kind of life anymore, and there were no other relatives to go to.

Right from the start, Austin had wanted to *be* like Uncle Drayton with all his masculine traits—especially after he overheard him talking about Austin's father, Wesley Hutchinson. He could still scrunch his eyes shut tight and hear it, Uncle Drayton telling Aunt Olivia that Austin was just like his father, that "sniveling, whining Wesley."

"The poor child," Uncle Drayton had said about Austin, *"is following in the footsteps of a person so wrapped up in his noble causes he hasn't time to be a man himself, much less teach his son how to be one."*

Of course, since then Austin had learned to be just who he really was and to like himself that way. Even Uncle Drayton had told him he was turning into the best kind of man. And he'd learned some things about Uncle Drayton that had convinced Austin that he didn't really want to be just like him.

But right now, seeing him sitting so tall in his saddle—and even seeing Jefferson becoming a fine horseman—and certainly always being beaten at everything physical by Henry-James—he had to wonder, *Am I always just going to be bookish and nothing more?*

The question was like a storm rumbling way far off. It wasn't enough to make his lightning flash. It just gave him that shoulder-pinching feeling, which tightened as he suddenly felt Uncle Drayton's eyes on him.

"Austin, whatever has happened to your face?" he asked.

Austin ignored his own scrapes as he felt himself go red.

"No need to answer," Uncle Drayton said. A smile twitched at the corners of his lips. "You're out here being Austin, likely as not."

With another almost-smile, Uncle Drayton trotted off easily on the gelding, toward the rice fields, where the slaves were preparing the fields for the next planting. Polly was scowling after him. Even though she was much better-looking than she used to be, when thin-faced Polly scowled, it wasn't pretty.

"I don't get a minute's peace anymore," she said. "Mama is forever calling me, now that I'm the eldest."

"No, you're not," Charlotte said. She narrowed her eyes at Polly. "Kady is still the eldest."

"Do you see Kady around here?" Polly said. "I'm the oldest one *here*—and in Mama's eyes—"

"Hush up!" Charlotte said.

Tot edged in nervously, but Polly sniffed. "Come on, Tot," she said. "We have things to do. Let her stay here and moon over Kady if she wants. I sure thought there was going to be more peace around here with her gone, but there *isn't*."

She went off toward the Big House, muttering to Tot, who

listened to every word, happy just to be with her mistress. Austin took a glance at Charlotte.

Of all of them, Charlotte was the one who seemed to miss her oldest sister Kady the most. Kady had run off and married a man who was "below the station" of the Ravenals without telling her parents. Ever since then, Aunt Olivia wouldn't even let her in the house. Kady and Fitzgerald lived on the outskirts of Charleston— and only Charlotte, Austin, and Henry-James knew that she and her new husband were helping slaves escape from their masters to freedom in the North.

"So *now* what are we going to do?" Jefferson said. "I'm *bored*!"

"What do you *want*?" Austin said. "We just had a horse race. We've been entertaining you all morning."

"That's what you're supposed to do," Jefferson said. He punctuated that with a firm nod of his dark head.

"I didn't think you were like that anymore, Jefferson," Charlotte said. "I thought you'd learned how to amuse yourself."

"I hate amusing myself," Jefferson said. "It's boring."

"You're boring," Austin said.

Immediately, Jefferson's tongue whipped out, and he waggled it at Austin. Austin made a dive to grab for it, but Henry-James stuck out a casual arm and held Austin back. Jefferson squealed and made a beeline for the bay mare.

She whinnied nervously as Jefferson thrust a foot into the stirrup, grabbed up a handful of mane, and with a spring popped himself into the saddle.

"What you doin', Massa Jefferson?" Henry-James called out over his shoulder.

"Taking this horse back to the stable," he said. "I can."

It looked as if he could. He gave the reins a yank, and the mare reluctantly turned her head and moved toward the barnyard area.

"Wait!" Charlotte said. "I'll come with you."

"I can do it myself."

"I know. I just want to come with you."

Charlotte scrambled over the hedge to the blood bay and started him moving before she was all the way on. Both horses took off back down the buggy path with dust kicking up behind them.

Henry-James put his hand over his mouth and nose and looked at Austin.

"Come on, Massa Austin," he said. "I gots to get you to Mama and get you fixed up 'fore you bleeds to death."

"I'm not going to bleed to death," Austin said sullenly.

"I can't take no chances," he said. "'Sides, that's my job. I done tol' Marse Drayton—"

"I know, I know." Austin pulled his arm away from Henry-James, but he walked dutifully beside him, kicking miserably at the dirt. Bogie trailed behind, constantly sniffing the ground with his wet nose, his ears making paths in the sand.

"You sure are being the model slave lately, Henry-James," Austin said.

"Uh-huh. I done promised Daddy 'Lias."

Daddy Elias was Henry-James's grandfather, and Austin had loved him almost as much as Henry-James himself had. If Henry-James had promised the old man before he died that he would be a model slave and not cause Uncle Drayton any trouble, then he had to stick to it. Unless, of course, "Marse Jesus" seemed to have another path for him. They'd both learned that just this past winter.

"Let me ask you this, Massa Austin," Henry-James said suddenly.

"What?" Austin said.

Henry-James cocked his shiny head in the sunlight and ran his tongue through the gap between his teeth. "You think that there Abraham Lincoln—you think he gonna free the slaves now he's got himself . . . what you call it?"

"Inaugurated?" Austin said.

"That means he president now?"

"Right."

"Yeah—that."

Austin wished he could say yes—that he could say it were already so and that Henry-James could fly like one of their great blue herons right then. But he frowned down at the sandy path as they crossed through the back garden toward the Big House.

"I don't think so," Austin said. "I've been reading the *Charleston Mercury* every day. Mr. Lincoln, in his speech he had to make at his inauguration, you know—"

"Uh-huh."

"He said he was going to leave slavery alone in the states that already had slaves. But he said he has to uphold the national authority."

"What's that there mean?"

"It means states can't be breaking away—seceding like they have here in the South. He says he doesn't want any bloodshed, but he'll defend the Union—that's the country, the United States— if he has to."

Henry-James grunted. "He ain't defending *me* if'n he don't set me free."

Austin looked at him sideways. "And that's the only way you're going to be free, isn't it, Henry-James? If there's a law that says you are."

"Daddy 'Lias, he tol' me it ain't so bad. He say Uncle Drayton, he don't treat us like no animals—we's people to him—not like some massas."

Out over the river, there was a low mumble, coming from the sky. Bogie whined and hurried to plaster himself to Henry-James's side.

"Ain't nothin' but thunder, Bogie," Henry-James said.

"And it isn't even that loud yet," Austin said. "It's just now muttering under its breath."

Henry-James shook his head. "That don't make no never

mind to Bogie. He know it gonna grumble itself right into a roar and then a crash and then a big ol' fit."

It was Austin's turn to grunt. "Just like Jefferson does when he gets worked up."

"Just like Marse Drayton," Henry-James said. And then he concentrated on getting Austin to the Big House before the rain came.

Ria, Henry-James's tall, sparely-made mother, was as usual in Sally Hutchinson's room, tending to her health. When she saw Austin, she put her hands to the waistline of her full-skirted dress and shook her scarf-covered head.

"Austin, what on earth!" Mother cried from her place in the brocade chair by the fireplace. "Have you been in a fight with someone?"

Ria took hold of one of Austin's shoulders and stared him straight in the face, her mouth tightening into a line.

"You done fell and went sprawlin' is what you done," Ria said. "Ain't that right, now?"

"I came off a horse," Austin said.

Mother arched her deer-colored Ravenal eyebrows, and Austin could see her trying not to smile. "You were riding?" she said.

"With Charlotte," Austin said. "She took a jump and I . . . I just came off."

"You wasn't hangin' on, is what," Ria said.

She walked toward him with a bowl of water and a cloth, and Austin knew better than to move away as she pushed him down into the chair opposite his mother. But he scowled as Ria went after his sore cheek with the wet cloth. He'd rather not go back to *this* subject.

"Is he all right, Ria?" Mother said.

"I'm all right," Austin said. "I can answer for myself."

Mother's eyebrows went up again, her big eyes widening in her pale face, and Austin knew he'd been rude. He felt stupid.

She let her look linger on him for another moment, and then she let it pass.

"I'm glad you came in. I wanted to show you the letter I'm sending to your father today," she said.

Austin twisted his mouth. He'd known this was coming again. It was only a matter of time now with the trouble between the North and the South getting worse and worse. Lincoln's inauguration speech had practically been a declaration of war, as far as the Southrons were concerned.

But there was still that special something Austin needed to do. He didn't know what yet—but they had tried to leave so many times before and hadn't been able to, and Austin was sure it was because Jesus still had something for him to do here. He'd felt it so strongly.

"I know we've tried before," Mother was saying, "but now your father really has to find a way to get us back to the North. I want us out before the war starts in earnest."

Austin sighed and watched Ria wash his elbow.

"I just wanted you to be ready," Mother said. "I don't know how your father will do it—we've tried several different ways— but he'll do it. He'll find a way for us to get out."

"Of course he will," Austin said.

His mother nodded and stood up. "Why don't I pour us both some tea? Ria was just getting it ready."

She stepped lightly across the room to the tea cart. Austin turned his attention back to the job Ria was doing on his other arm.

But she'd stopped washing, and she was watching Mother's back like a mother hen clucking after her chicks.

"Wesley Hutchinson ought to come down here himself and fetch his family," she said under her breath. "That what a man oughta do."

✝━◆━✝

Chapter Three

𝕴n a fraction of a second, Ria was back to washing his elbow, and Austin was blinking, trying to decide if she had actually said it.

She must have. Her eyes were glued to her hands. If Tot hadn't chosen that moment to fling the door open, he wasn't sure what he might have said.

"Well, Tot honey, why don't you just come on in?" Sally Hutchinson said.

She grinned as poor befuddled Tot scrunched her forehead in the direction of the door as if to say, "Didn't I just do that? Didn't I just come in?"

Ria wiped her hands briskly on the cloth and swished over to Tot. "Girl, what on earth have you got goin' on with your skirt?"

Tot looked guiltily over at her own backside and hunched her head down into her shoulders.

Austin's mother laughed. "You look like you're wearing an entire turkey under there, Tot. What is that?"

Ria didn't wait for an answer. She reached up under Tot's crisp house uniform and yanked out two feather dusters. Tot's head nearly disappeared into her shoulder blades.

"What you doin' wearin' the missus' dusters under your dress, girl?"

Tot muttered something none of them heard.

"Speak up, girl!" Ria said.

"It's all right, Tot," Mother said. "You're not in trouble." She patted Tot's arm. "You can tell us. Were you playing some kind of game?"

Ria gave a sniff.

Tot looked pleadingly at Sally Hutchinson. "I was havin' me a bustle," she said—in that voice that always sounded to Austin like someone dragging a fingernail across a tin pail. It sent a shiver up his spine.

"A bustle?" Ria said. "Now what in the name of heaven is *that*?"

"We done seen 'em in Miz Polly's catalog!" Tot cried, voice winding up even further. "All them rich ladies got 'em."

"Then it's sure that's who should be wearin' them—not you," Ria said. She pulled out Tot's hands and slapped both feather dusters into them. "Now go do what you supposed to be doin' with these."

Tot turned to go, but Mother caught her by the arm. She couldn't speak for a moment, though. Her whole face was twitching with held-back laughter. "What did you come in here for, Tot?" she said. "Surely you weren't going to dust my room with your derriere?"

Tot shook her head, and then just stood there with her mouth hanging open. Austin couldn't help rolling his eyes.

"So what *did* you come in for?" Mother said.

"Supper," Tot said. She broke into a sloppy smile and nodded enthusiastically. "That's it. You gots to come to supper—Miz 'Livia say."

"Should I wear my bustle?" Mother said.

Tot grinned happily.

"Austin, too?" his mother said.

"I don't think so!" Austin cried.

Mother laughed and held out her arm to him. "No one could mistake you for a girl anyway, my fine son."

Austin grunted. She seemed to be the only one who thought so—about him *or* his father.

When they reached the dining room downstairs, Jefferson was just skidding in, reeking of horse smells—leather, sweat, urine, and manure. Aunt Olivia already had a hanky over her plump face and was shooing him out with the flounced cuff of her long lace sleeve. The puffs of hair over her ears were near to standing straight out on end, and although Austin couldn't see her mouth, he was sure her two-going-on-three chins were jiggling.

"You may *not* come to my table smelling like that!" she was nearly shouting.

"Upstairs with you, Jefferson," Mother said. Once again, she was smothering a grin. "We'll send something up to the nursery, all right?"

"I want Kady to bring it," Jefferson said.

"Don't be foolish, child," Aunt Olivia said. "You know she isn't here."

"When's she coming back?"

"She isn't! Why are you asking me the same questions I answered for you yesterday—and the day before that?"

Aunt Olivia's chins were fully visible now, and they were as scarlet-pink as the rest of her face. Uncle Drayton, who was standing behind his chair at the head of the table, ran his hand across his freshly brushed hair and flicked his wrist at Tot.

"Fetch the boy a tray and take it up to the nursery," he said. "Tot will do, won't she, little man?"

Jefferson shrugged and latched on to Tot's apron. As long as his hero Uncle Drayton suggested it, it was fine. Austin felt an old stab of resentment. Jefferson was the little man—Uncle Drayton's favorite—the one who could outride Austin at age seven and—

"Sit, sit, sit, all of you!" Aunt Olivia said fretfully. "The food will be cold and not fit to eat."

Actually, Austin hadn't tasted much at this table that wasn't "fit to eat." Josephine was an amazing cook as far as he was concerned. Usually Austin's mouth would have been watering as Josephine put the chicken with corn pudding on the table and they all waited while Henry-James, now dressed in his plush house servant clothes, spread the linen napkin in Uncle Drayton's lap.

But tonight Austin barely tasted the pudding. All he could think about was what Ria had said about his father—that he wasn't man enough to come into the South, where he was now considered to be the enemy for being against slavery, and take his wife and children back home.

And that must mean I'm the same, he thought. *I thought I was all settled on being what Jesus meant for me to be.*

But what if that isn't what I want to be?

Henry-James had been right. The muttering of thunder in the distance did often grumble itself into a roar—no matter whether it was a real storm or one inside Austin. Right now, though, Aunt Olivia's shrill voice drowned even that out.

"I, for one, am glad to hear it," she was saying.

Austin knew she must be talking about the letter his mother was sending to his father. She'd wanted the Hutchinsons to leave before they'd even arrived.

"After all," she went on, "there is bound to be a war, and you certainly don't want to be stuck here!"

"Now, Olivia, I wish you wouldn't say things like that," Uncle Drayton said. He dabbed at his mustache with his napkin and waited for Henry-James to rearrange it in his lap. "I don't think war is inevitable at all. You children listen to this."

Charlotte looked up from her plate as if, like Austin, she had been a million miles away. "Yes, Daddy," she said.

"Oh," Polly said, "I think a war would be awfully romantic. I love men in uniform."

"You love men in anything," Charlotte mumbled.

Austin couldn't help grinning at her across the table. She grinned back and then pretended to be interested in her cornbread.

"There are other ways to settle this ridiculous rift," Uncle Drayton went on.

"I think you're wrong," Austin's mother said. "Look at what's happening. Texas has joined the Confederacy now, which brings the total of states to seven. And federal forts and navy yards in all seven have been seized by the CSA—"

"What is the CSA?" Polly said.

"Confederate States of America," Austin rattled off.

"Thank you. Go on."

"One of the only forts in the South that's still in Union hands is Fort Sumter—right out there in the Charleston harbor," Sally Hutchinson said. "You don't think that Brigadier General P.G.T. Beauregard has taken command of the Confederate troops in Charleston just so he can wear a fancy uniform and impress Polly, do you?"

"Wouldn't that be nice, though?" Polly said.

Austin and Charlotte rolled their eyes at each other. At 14, men were all Polly could seem to think about.

"No," Mother said. "He's fortifying the harbor, Drayton. Fort Sumter is the focal point of the tensions between the North and the South. That certainly sounds like war to me."

"Only if your Major Anderson out there on Sumter refuses to leave. The Confederates have asked him to take his men off the island, you know."

"And you think if he does it there won't be any gunfire?" she said.

"I know so." Uncle Drayton shook his handsome head. "The South won't need to fight if we have what we want, which is to control our own future."

Austin still had a hard time getting used to hearing Uncle Drayton talk as if he were a member of the Confederacy. Sure, Uncle Drayton approved of slavery—he had 600 slaves of his own. And he loved the kind of life the plantation owners had carved out for themselves in the South. But right up to the day that secession had been declared, he hadn't thought the South should separate from the rest of the country, and he had suffered the loss of friends and even some attacks because he wouldn't join in with the Fire Eaters who finally formed the Confederate States.

He'd made up his mind, though, and it made Austin cringe. There was sure to be an argument now between Uncle Drayton and his sister, Sally. Austin had heard Aunt Olivia say a number of times to Polly that she liked it much better when Sally was too sick to debate at the table.

Sure enough, Austin's mother sat up like a pole in her chair. "Control of the future so it can continue to have all the slaves it wants," she said. There was no twinkle in her eyes. The family shine faded from Uncle Drayton's, too.

"I don't want to go over this with you again, Sally," he said. "The greatest legal minds in the United States decided once and for all—four years ago—that black people do not fall under the law and therefore we can do with them as we please."

"There is a higher law, Drayton. We've talked about this. God's law is above the Constitution. No matter what the Constitution— yours or ours—says, slavery is against the higher law."

"That is nothing but abolitionist talk."

"We abolitionists are right!"

"You think you are—we think we are. We should leave each other alone to act on what we believe."

Sally Hutchinson pushed her chair back from the table and

leaned on it, her face pale in the flickering lamp light.

"If we 'leave you alone'," she said, "there will never be an end to slavery. And that is the worst thing I can think of." She nodded to Aunt Olivia. "Will you excuse me?"

Without waiting for an answer, she plucked up her skirts and hurried out of the room. There wasn't a sound in the dining room as they listened to her light footsteps disappear up the stairs.

"Pass the rice, would you, please, Polly dear?" Aunt Olivia said.

Austin lifted his lip. How could she go on and eat when her husband had just sent Austin's mother crying out of the room?

Austin let his own fork clatter to his plate.

How can I eat? I should go over there and slug Uncle Drayton right in the mouth, for upsetting her like that!

But he couldn't. And for that he didn't know whom he disliked more—Uncle Drayton or himself.

"Austin!" said a loud voice from the doorway.

Austin turned around and looked at Jefferson. He was standing there with corn pudding smeared on one cheek, shifting his weight from one foot to the other.

"What?" Austin said.

"I have to go to the necessary. I don't want Tot going out there with me—she's a girl!"

"Oh, I am *scan*dalized!" Aunt Olivia cried. "Such talk at the *table!*"

"Why can't you go by yourself, shrimp?" Austin said.

"Because . . . it's dark."

"Oh, for heaven's sake, don't be a 'fraidy cat!" Polly said.

"You'd be afraid, too, if you'd been readin' Brothers Grimm!"

Austin groaned. "I thought Mother told you not to read those scary stories anymore."

"Were you reading them to Tot?" Polly said. "Now she'll have me up all night!"

"I have to *go*, Austin!" Jefferson said.

"Take that child out of here!" Aunt Olivia said.

"Austin, please," Uncle Drayton said. "Henry-James, you accompany the boys. Make sure there's a fire going out there."

Austin got up and grabbed Jefferson by the arm. Henry-James came up on the other side and they lifted Jefferson out of the dining room, through the big back hall, and down the back steps. Once Jefferson got to this point, it was usually best to get him to the necessary as fast as possible.

The necessary was a small building behind the Big House with three long benches and seven holes. It was March-night chilly in there, and Henry-James went right over to the fireplace and got some kindling lit while Austin lifted Jefferson up onto one of the high benches. Jefferson's feet dangled with his pants hanging down over his ankles.

Austin leaned against the bench and angrily crossed his arms.

"I wanted so bad to hit Uncle Drayton for making Mother cry like that," he said.

Henry-James grunted from the fireplace.

"Don't you ever want to just . . . let him have it?" Austin said.

"Not no more," he said. "Not since what Daddy 'Lias tol' me on his dyin' day."

"What did he say?" Austin said. "Exactly."

Henry-James pushed a log into the fireplace and watched the flames lick around it as if they were tasting it.

"He tol' me to remember that it ain't us that's got to get vengeance on people like Marse Drayton," he said. "The Lord, He gonna take care all that."

"What are you supposed to do in the meantime, while Uncle Drayton's going on about how you aren't good enough to be protected by laws and all that?"

"I's s'posed to remember that those that's suffered most on earth gonna be rewarded in heaven. Plus, the good Lord give me strength to do what I gots to do now."

Austin considered that while Henry-James put another log on the fire. It looked like Jefferson was going to be there for a while.

"Did Daddy Elias learn all that in church?" Austin said finally.

"No, sir," Henry-James said. "That white preacher—that Reverend Pullens—he a mighty good preacher and he can sure 'nuff tell a Bible story—"

"Not like Daddy Elias, though."

"No—and he only say what the white marse like Marse Drayton want to hear."

"What do you mean?" Austin said.

Henry-James didn't take his eyes off the fire, and Austin watched them. They glowed hot and angry, like the flames.

"That there Reverend Pullens, he all the time sayin' God made us black folk for to be slaves, so we got to be nice to our massa and missus and be obedient and work hard, 'cause when we sin against the massa, we sinnin' against God."

"He says Uncle Drayton is like God?" Austin said. "Huh!"

"You know all them things Marse Jesus say in the Bible 'bout bein' servants like He is?" Henry-James said.

"Yes," Austin said.

"That there preacher, he tell us we got to be servants cheerful-like, and not just when the marse be watchin'. He say Jesus done that, so we got to, too. He say we ain't sufferin' no more than the Lord did."

Austin stood up straight and marched over to the fireplace. He squatted down to face Henry-James. "Did Daddy Elias believe that?"

"No, sir," Henry-James said. He was still staring into the fire with his eyes glittering. "But he say if'n I's good to Marse Drayton and I prays for him, he gonna treat me better and the Lord gonna reward me, just like He done him."

"But didn't we talk about how Jesus has a different path for each of us? Didn't I tell you that the minute I got back to Charleston when we almost left—"

"You did," Henry-James said. "And I believe you right, Massa Austin. I sure tryin' to do what Daddy 'Lias tol' me, but my heart, it ain't in it like it was for him."

"You know why?" Austin said.

"No."

"Because I think you're going to go free, Henry-James."

Henry-James shook his head.

"Why not?" Austin said.

"You don't think I be listenin' when Miz Sally and Marse Drayton be arguin' like that?"

He looked Austin in the eye for the first time. "What Jesus want for me ain't gonna happen, Massa Austin. Not for Henry-James."

·I·┿·I·

Chapter Four

After his talk with Henry-James, the thunder seemed to mutter louder in Austin's chest. And it seemed every other hour over the next few days, lightning was flickering in the distance, too.

For one thing, Aunt Olivia couldn't seem to stop barking at Polly, and, of course, Tot.

When Polly and Tot were sitting out beyond the bamboo grove among the azaleas, and Polly was reading *Malaesha: the Indian Wife of the White Hunter* out loud to Tot, Aunt Olivia sent Mousie out to find them. Aunt Olivia screeched for an hour about how Polly was going to twist her mind reading those cheap dime novels.

Another day Aunt Olivia caught Tot rubbing milk into Polly's skin to prevent wrinkles, and Aunt Olivia hollered about them wasting precious food when a war was about to start. Austin didn't see what that had to do with anything—the soldiers weren't going to shoot each other with milk.

When Aunt Olivia was going out to the storeroom one Saturday afternoon to ration food to the slaves for the week—with Mousie following behind her with the basket full of keys—Tot came barreling across the lawn with a Venus's-flytrap in her hand, shouting to Polly that she'd found a plant that had a mouth. She plowed right into Mousie, dumping the basket and sending keys flying like startled moths. Aunt Olivia was so angry that she made Tot get down on her hands and knees and find every one *while* she was screaming at Polly for not keeping her slave girl under control. Austin himself went looking for the Venus's-flytrap. He'd heard it could capture insects with its leaves and then give off a juice that turned the bug into food, but he'd never actually seen one.

And as if all of that weren't bad enough, Uncle Drayton was taking his tensions out on Henry-James. The silver braid on Henry-James's uniform wasn't straight when he drove the family to church in the coach. The coffee he brought to Uncle Drayton in bed was too hot. The iron he used to press Uncle Drayton's pants was too cold. He found a spot on his boots, a tick on one of his hounds, a scratch on his best saddle—and it was all Henry-James's fault.

Austin couldn't laugh at any of that.

And he certainly didn't find the fact that Jefferson was in rare form very funny either.

"He was doing so well for a while," Charlotte said one day when Henry-James dragged the little boy in dripping wet from tumbling into the reflection pool in the gardens.

"He's not doing well now," Austin said. "He's acting like a spoiled little brat again."

One day he pulled a bunch of Spanish moss off the oak trees and draped it over his head to pretend he was a crazy old hermit with wild hair, parading through the house. The moss was infested with fleas. Jefferson wasn't the only one who itched for days.

The next day he ran through the laundry yard where the slave women had just hung all the clothes out to dry on the clotheslines. He caught onto a set of Uncle Drayton's long underdrawers and flew across the plantation with the legs flying out behind him like a cape. Bogie thought that was a wonderful game and grabbed the drawers with his teeth. Uncle Drayton was left with only fringe from the knees down.

While Tot was watching Jefferson, he jumped up onto Polly's bed and took a knife to it until down from her featherbed filled the room like snow. And he pulled the bell pull so many times one day that even patient Josephine's eyes began to bulge in anger. Austin tied Jefferson's hands behind his back that day, until his mother made him take the ropes off.

"Don't you feel all the tension in the air?" Mother said to him when Jefferson had run off crying to his room.

"Yes," Austin said.

"Well, so does he. Only he doesn't know what to do with it, so he goes out and does crazy-dog things."

"Tell that to everybody else," Austin said. "He knocked over the oil lamp in Uncle Drayton's library. He walked in on Polly when she was having a bath in the kitchen—"

"I know," his mother said. "And I know it's wrong. But let me take care of him, all right? No more binding and gagging."

"Gagging," Austin said. "I didn't think of that!"

It would have been an unbearable couple of weeks while they waited for Wesley Hutchinson's reply and waited for Major Anderson to leave Fort Sumter and waited for Abraham Lincoln or Jefferson Davis to declare war—if it hadn't been for Charlotte. Henry-James was busy with Uncle Drayton and Polly with her mother, and Jefferson was always being sent to his room for wreaking havoc on the whole plantation, so the two of them were left on their own to find things to do.

And they did.

On the days when the spring storms came—almost every other day—they stayed inside and played checkers and dominos and worked jigsaw puzzles.

But as soon as the sun came out, they were off looking for adventures.

At the sundial in the rose garden, they pretended they were great scholars studying time. That was Austin's idea.

Down at the biggest live oak on the river, Charlotte showed him the markings the Indians had left there long before the white man came to South Carolina. Since the live oak dropped its leaves in the spring, too, big piles of green ones, they had plenty of materials for making hiding places and pretend teepees and canoes. It turned into an Indian adventure that lasted three days. That was Austin's idea, too.

But it was Charlotte's idea that turned into the most interesting game. They were wandering in the formal gardens with Bogie around mid-March, finally bored with being chief and squaw, when Charlotte pointed to the north end of the reflection pond.

"Do you want to go down that path, Austin?" she said.

Bogie sniffed curiously.

"What path?" Austin said.

"Come on. You have to get closer to see it. I'll show you."

Licking his chops with delicious anticipation, Austin followed her to a thick hedge of holly, Bogie trotting along behind him.

"I still don't see a path," he said.

"You have to be a friend of the forest to see it," Charlotte said. Her eyes were sparkling, and she deepened her voice even lower than usual.

"Friend of the forest?" Austin said. "That would be me, all right. I know all the Latin names, you know. Live oak is *quercus virginiana*—"

"I know, I know," Charlotte said. She tossed her hair back over her shoulders. "Not that kind of friend. More like a *real* friend. You know, like you and I are."

"What do you mean?"

"You see things in a friend that nobody else sees, right?" she said.

"Sure, I guess."

"So it's the same with the woods. If you aren't a friend, you see only a bunch of trees, some moss, and you think, *Oh, what if I get lost in there?* But if you're a *friend* of the forest, it will tell you its secrets."

He watched as she got down on her hands and knees, impatiently shoving her plaid skirts out behind her, and crawled low to the ground. Bogie got down beside her, whimpering in concern.

"What are you doing?" Austin said.

"I have to see where the holly bushes are planted farther apart—here it is!"

She stuck up her hand and waved Austin down. He dropped to his knees and peered down where she was pointing while Bogie licked his ears. She hadn't been fooling. There was a narrow, sandy path, winding down from the holly bushes.

With one wiggle she was on the other side of the hedge, Bogie with her. With a series of grunts and moans, Austin got himself between the trunks with only a poke or two from some holly leaves. Charlotte put her hand down to help him up, but he ignored it and got to his feet.

"Where does it go?" Austin said.

"How would I know?" Charlotte said.

"Haven't you ever been down it?"

She shook her head, deer-colored hair going everywhere. "No. I've been waiting for just the right friend at just the right time." She grinned again. "And I think this is it."

It was as if some giant hand came out and stilled his storm. He forgot the almost-war, the screaming and yelling going on back at the Big House, and even the fact that he and his father were supposedly the weaklings of all mankind. There was sun, there was Bogie slobbering on his hand, and there was Charlotte, who didn't care if he wasn't the strongest boy in South Carolina.

"Let's go," he said.

At first they decided it was a country owned by elves—what with the zany-looking spider lilies and the mischievous Venus's-flytraps lining the path. But then suddenly the trees started meeting over them, forming a shady tunnel that only tiny dapples of sunlight could penetrate. Beyond the tunnel, the oaks and pine, cypress and sweetgum, poplar and hickory grew dense and thick.

"Let's pretend this is part of the Underground Railroad," Austin whispered.

"And Harriet Tubman herself is waiting over there in the ferns for her next maroon."

"That would be us," Austin said. "We've just run away from Canaan Grove, and we're trying to escape the evil hound."

Charlotte looked doubtfully down at Bogie, who was wagging his tail and drooling on the path.

"And the problem is, I can't see very well," Austin said. "I've been locked in solitary confinement with no light and just enough air to breathe."

"Oh, that's right," she said. "If it weren't for the corn muffins and okra I've been sneaking you, you'd be dead. Come, I'll have to lead you."

She took hold of his arm, and they darted off down the path. Bogie stood for a moment, looking confused, and then loped after them.

"We'll never get away from him this way," Charlotte said. "Not unless we get to some water. Dogs can't track in the water, you know."

Austin opened his "blind eyes" and looked at her. "Oh, they lose the scent, huh?"

"Right. We'll have to find a swamp to dive into."

Austin slammed his eyes shut again. "All right, I can do that. You just lead the way."

But as they moved on, with Bogie happily unaware that he was an evil tracking animal, Austin snuck a glance up at the trees. He'd heard that cottonmouth snakes liked to hang up there and drop on people.

"If we can just get away from this killer dog, we'll be fine," Charlotte whispered.

"Sure," Austin said, eyes closed again. "Until we're captured by slave hunters or gobbled up by alligators or accidentally eat a poison mushroom—"

"But none of that is going to happen."

"You can never tell. I bet a lot of slaves that have tried to escape have—"

"It won't happen," she said.

Austin opened his eyes. She was looking him in the face, her eyes dull and flat as a pair of rocks.

"Why?" Austin said.

"Just because. That's too . . . awful."

"Oh." Austin shrugged. *What good is a game if nothing awful happens in it?* he thought.

"Wait!"

Charlotte stopped so suddenly in front of him that he ran up her heel and had to stumble sideways to keep from falling flat.

"What?" he said.

Charlotte put her finger up to her lips and pointed ahead of them.

Austin looked, but he didn't see anything except more of the path and the woods, with shafts of sunlight filtering through. Bogie, however, went crashing through the bushes—and came out with his tail flapping.

"There's something in there," she said. "Listen!"

Austin cocked his head, and at first there was nothing but the gentle creaking sound of the tree limbs rubbing together. He shook his head at Charlotte. She took his arm and guided him to the side of the path, near the plum thicket. He pulled up his elbows to keep from getting pricked by the thorns and looked where she pointed.

He heard something before he saw what she did. There was a soft humming—a song Austin had heard the slaves sing in the fields before, but this time without the words.

And then he spotted someone between the spindly branches. It was Tot, crouched down with her head bent over something, humming in fits and starts like a distracted bird.

Charlotte and Austin looked at each other with question marks in their eyes. Bogie gave up and lay down. Austin returned his gaze to Tot.

Where's Polly? he thought. *I didn't think Tot could* breathe *without Polly telling her to.*

Charlotte poked Austin in the side and pulled him by the sleeve to peek around the thin trunk of a sapling. From that angle, he could see what Tot was doing, and once again he furrowed his forehead at Charlotte.

Charlotte shrugged and kept studying the stumpy slave girl. Tot, between stanzas of her humming-song, was carefully selecting mushrooms from a stand of them that was clustered like tables in a hotel dining room. Austin watched as she plucked one and held it up to her nose and interrupted her humming to give a loud sniff. Then she examined its underside and tugged at its stem and finally dropped it into the pocket of her apron.

The pocket was already bulging as if several were in there, but not all had survived the choosing. Just as many were lying on the ground beside her, stems up and caps already shriveling.

Austin poked Charlotte and mouthed to her, "What is she doing?"

Charlotte shook her head and then held Austin's wrist. Tot

had stopped humming and was getting up. She shook out her apron, losing two of the mushrooms from the pocket in the process. She hummed in a higher octave as she leaned over, picked them up, blew on them, and stuck them back in with the others. Then being careful not to step on the ones she'd rejected, she picked her way out of the dark, soggy clearing and headed back for the path.

It wasn't hard to know when Tot was out of earshot. She hummed happily and rattled bushes and scattered leaves all the way back to the gardens near the Big House, as far as Austin could tell.

"What in the world was that all about?" Austin said.

"Why didn't we ask her?"

"What?"

Charlotte was smiling strangely. "Why didn't we just ask her? We were hiding in the thicket like we didn't want her to see us."

Austin grinned. "Of course not. We're slaves, trying to escape. We're not going to stop everybody we see and *tell* them!"

Charlotte shook her head. "I think I don't want to play that game anymore, Boston."

"Why not?"

"I don't want to think about slaves escaping. I mean . . ." She sighed at the ground. "Just not *our* slaves."

"You wouldn't want Henry-James to be free? He could do anything he wanted then. Read any book, wear any clothes—"

"I don't want to talk about it," she said.

"Why not?"

"I just don't. Race you back."

And she was already gone, skittering off down the path like a deer, with Bogie bounding after her. Austin followed at a flailing run. It somehow felt as if he were running from the sound of thunder that was coming nearer and nearer.

✛·✛·✛

Chapter Five

Things were uneasy at the dinner table again that after-noon. Austin only half listened to the bickering and whining as he examined the okra stew to see if there were any mushrooms in it.

Some of them make good eating. I read about that, he thought. *But you have to be careful. The wrong one can kill you!*

"Drayton," Aunt Olivia said, "that *boy* has been at it again."

Uncle Drayton gave her an amused grin over a spoonful of stew. "I assume you mean our little man, Jefferson."

"I fail to see the humor!" she cried, chins wobbling. "He had his hands in the brown sugar barrel all morning."

"He was probably looking for lumps to eat," Uncle Drayton said. "We've all done that."

He's in a good mood, Austin thought. He glanced up at Henry-James, who was standing still against the wall behind Uncle Drayton's chair. A good mood for Uncle Drayton meant a good day for Henry-James—although it was hard to tell from his face. He never moved it when he was waiting on his master. He wasn't allowed to have feelings of his own when he was supposed to be thinking of Uncle Drayton's, Austin had figured out.

"Drayton and I used to have contests to see who could find

the biggest lump," Austin's mother was saying.

"Looking for candy is fine," Aunt Olivia said. "But not with the same hands that have been helping deliver kittens in the barn!"

Polly choked on her sugar muffin. Tot leaped forward to rescue her and knocked over a dish of peach preserves that spread like mud across the lace tablecloth. Mousie dove in to wipe it up, and Aunt Olivia flapped her hands in front of her crimson face. Austin had never seen the chins move quite that fast.

"Tot, you oaf!" she cried. "Polly, she is an absolute ox! How on earth will you ever run a household with that bovine beside you? Mousie, stop wiping that table and fetch my handkerchief. I may faint!"

"It wasn't her fault!" Polly screeched back. "You were the one who nearly made me gag with all that talk of wretched little hands in our food!"

"My child is not wretched!" said Sally Hutchinson. "I don't know how you expect him to behave with the atmosphere that exists in this house—"

"Enough!" Uncle Drayton shouted.

He was using his trumpet voice, the one that jolted everybody to silence when he blared it out. Austin sneaked a look across the table at Charlotte, who wiggled an eyebrow at him. When they weren't the ones being yelled at, it was kind of fun to listen to one of Uncle Drayton's tirades.

"I'll thank you not to raise your voice at me, Drayton," Aunt Olivia said. "I'm not strong these days."

"Poppycock, Livvy," Uncle Drayton said. "You're strong as an . . . well, you're strong. We all are. What we need is to get away from all this endless thinking about war and such."

What else are we supposed to think about? Austin thought. *That's all anybody talks about.*

It was something Kady might have said if she'd been there.

Austin suddenly missed her. But Uncle Drayton's next statement brushed that little piece of loneliness aside.

"We are going to Charleston," he said.

"Yes!" Polly said. She clapped her hands about 20 times, and Tot commenced to nodding happily behind her.

"Whatever for?" Aunt Olivia said.

"For the St. Patrick's Day parade," Uncle Drayton said.

"Do they still do that?" Mother said.

"Absolutely. Only it's better than ever," Uncle Drayton said. "I think it's the perfect thing to take our minds off our troubles."

Austin's mind was already heading in that direction. Any trip into the city of Charleston was an adventure as far as he was concerned—and now that Kady lived there, it was possible he might see her, too.

"When can we leave, Daddy?" Polly said.

"First thing in the morning. The parade is the day after tomorrow."

"Drayton, you've given me absolutely no time to prepare!" Aunt Olivia said.

"Nonsense," Uncle Drayton said. He pushed himself back from the table. "If we all begin now, we can be aboard the packet at dawn, headed for a good time."

"I don't see how I can possibly go, Drayton," Austin's mother said.

Austin felt himself deflating. Across the table, Charlotte gave him an anxious look.

"You need a distraction, too, sweet potato pie," Uncle Drayton said.

"I'm sure I do, but what if Wesley tries to get in touch with me while I'm in the city? Time could be precious if he finds a way to get us back to the North."

Austin wanted to stand up—*on* the table—and protest. As it was, he clung to the sides of the chair and said, "You just sent the letter. He probably hasn't even gotten it yet!"

Uncle Drayton glanced at him. "I think he's right, Sally. Besides, we're only going to be gone three days at the most. If a message does come, there will still be time."

But Austin's mother was shaking her head. Austin almost crawled across the table.

"It isn't safe for us there anyway; you know that," she said. "It wasn't two months ago that—"

She looked quickly at Austin and stopped. Now definitely wasn't a good time to bring up what had happened during the social season.

Austin looked helplessly from his mother to his uncle and back again. Uncle Drayton stroked his neat little beard until Austin thought he would scream.

"Then the Hutchinsons can stay here," Aunt Olivia said briskly. That seemed to make her like the thought of going to Charleston more. She stood up and flicked her hand at Mousie.

"No, I have an idea," Uncle Drayton said. "Sally, you stay here if it will make you feel better. Heaven knows you won't enjoy the parade if you're stewing over missing word from Wesley."

Austin held his breath.

"But there is no reason why Austin can't come along, is there? My sweet thing is lost without him, aren't you, my love?"

He smiled at Charlotte, who nodded even more enthusiastically than Tot.

Mother looked pained. Austin, for once, didn't trust himself to say anything.

"I don't know," she said. "I just fear for his safety—"

"Then I will put Henry-James in total charge of him," Uncle Drayton said. "Heaven knows he's probably more devoted to the boy than he is to me. He'll keep an eye on Austin every minute or he'll have me to answer to."

A strange resentment rose up in Austin.

"I don't need anybody to keep an eye on me every minute," he said. He could hear the unexpected tightness in his own voice. "I can look after myself."

"Well, then," Uncle Drayton said. The Ravenal twinkle was flashing in his eyes. "That must have been a rumor I heard about you falling off a horse a short while back—although how do you then explain the scabs I still see on your cheek there?"

"Haven't you ever fallen off a horse?" Austin said, words coiled like a spring.

"No," Uncle Drayton said. He gave his chin whiskers one more rub. "I don't think I have."

If there hadn't been the excitement of going to Charleston and seeing a parade to look forward to, Austin would have weathered that little squall for several days. But there was a bag to pack, and plans to make with Charlotte and Henry-James, and his mother to reassure.

"You remember what happened with those Fire Eaters," she whispered to him for the fifteenth time as she kissed him good-bye at the dock the next morning.

"Yes," he said. "And you remember how I got out of it, too."

"Thanks to Fitz. There isn't always going to be someone there to save you, Austin."

Austin moved his cheek away from her. "I don't always *need* someone to rescue me," he said.

After that, all they could hear were the sound of Jefferson shrieking to be allowed to go along—Aunt Olivia had absolutely put her foot down on that one—and Bogie howling because Henry-James was leaving him. Austin happily boarded Uncle Drayton's elegant packet boat and waved to a concerned Sally and a pouty Jefferson and a beside-himself Bogie as the Charleston-bound company started down the Ashley River.

It was usually a quiet trip, and Charlotte, Austin, Henry-James, and sometimes even Polly liked to pretend that they were the first settlers discovering the river. But that day, even the herons and the osprey seemed to be in a frenzy. The river was teeming with boats full of people shouting to each other across the water.

"You going to the parade?"

"It's going to be a lollapalooza!"

"Beauregard himself is marching in it!"

"Glory hallelujah! Honey, the South is gonna *rise*!"

"I thought it was supposed to be a St. Patrick's Day parade," Austin said to Charlotte.

"Doesn't sound like it to me," Henry-James mumbled.

And he was right.

The next day when the Ravenals and their personal slaves and Austin gathered with the rest of Charleston on Meeting Street, there was very little green being worn—and plenty of gray, the Confederate color.

Behind well-groomed oxen pulling cannons, soldiers marched in neat, proud lines wearing gray frock coats dripping with gold braid and sporting red silk sashes at their belts. The road was a sea of red, black-brimmed caps.

"They call them kepis," Austin told Charlotte. "I read that."

Polly didn't seem to care what their hats were called. She was enthralled even with the butternut-colored shell jackets worn by the cavalrymen.

"Oh dear, no, Polly," Aunt Olivia scolded her as she patted the lace favolet at the base of her bonnet. "You must set your sights on an officer. See there how that captain wears those gold epaulets?"

Austin and Charlotte exchanged rolling-eye looks.

"He's nothing but a dandy," Austin whispered to her. "He had that uniform made. See how it isn't like all the others?"

He was interrupted by a sudden roar from the crowd that only grew louder as the Charlestonians craned their necks to see down the street.

"What is it, Drayton?" Aunt Olivia cried, fanning her face on one side while Mousie fanned on the other.

Uncle Drayton frowned. "It looks to be General Beauregard himself."

"Catch me, Tot!" Polly cried. She plucked at the red and gray ribbons she'd fixed into her hair. "I think I'm going to faint!"

"She wishes," Charlotte muttered to Austin. "And she wishes he'd come along and revive her, too."

"He does have a pretty fancy uniform," Austin said.

General Pierre Gustave Toutant Beauregard was "pretty fancy" in every way possible, Austin decided as the Confederate commander was carried past on the shoulders of an adoring crowd of enlisted men. He sat as if he were in a grand carriage, elegantly waving his kepi at the crowd while not a hair on his dapper head moved in the breeze.

He shines it with macassar oil, Austin thought.

The general smiled in an even more charming manner than Uncle Drayton, and his thick mustache stayed as unruffled as his hair. But it was a crowd-pleasing smile, not a happy one. He didn't make Austin want to smile back.

"Oh, glory," Polly said, hardly breathing. "He is the finest of them all. Look at those gold buttons, those stars around his collar. Daddy, do you know him? Can't we go and visit him? I understand he's staying in that house right here on Meeting Street—the one that looks like a castle. It's so romantic."

Charlotte groaned out loud, and Austin laughed.

"Say something, Austin," Charlotte said, "so I don't have to listen to her anymore."

"General Beauregard is from Louisiana," Austin said. "He's a Creole. He's a gunner—in fact, he was such a good artillery student at West Point, his teacher kept him on as his assistant for another year."

"Do you know who that teacher was?" Uncle Drayton said.

Austin looked at him in surprise. "No," he said.

"Major Robert Anderson, the very man Beauregard is trying to run out of Fort Sumter."

There was a sadness in Uncle Drayton's voice that made Austin look at him twice. He shook his handsome head.

"If this does come to war the way all these people seem to hope it will, it will be a sad day," Uncle Drayton said. "A sad day indeed when teachers fight their students and fathers fight their sons, and brother and sister—"

A line of beating drums drowned him out. Austin fought off his own wave of sadness.

This really does mean I have to leave South Carolina, he thought. *It never seemed like it was going to happen before. Now it does. And I still haven't done what Jesus kept me here for.*

"Austin, look!" Charlotte suddenly burst out. "It's Kady!"

Austin followed her pointing finger as he looked across the street. As yet another line of infantrymen passed by, he saw her, too. She was dressed in a black bonnet and cape, and at the moment her usually rosy face was pale as a bowl of porridge.

"Did somebody die?" Austin said.

"What?" Charlotte said. Her eyes sparked with alarm.

"She looks so . . . I don't know . . . *sick*—"

Before he could finish his sentence, he knew why she looked as if she were bound for either a hospital or a funeral. A tall, gauntly thin man stepped out from behind her and glowered down at her with his eyebrows meeting in the middle like a pair of black caterpillars. It was Virgil Rhett, one of the Fire Eaters.

And if he was there, his cohorts Lawson Chesnut and Roger Pryor couldn't be far away. They'd been nothing but trouble for Uncle Drayton when he'd been struggling over whether to support the Southern states in their secession. And with the way Kady secretly felt about slavery, they were bound to be trouble for her, too.

"We should tell your father," Austin whispered to Charlotte.

But there was no need. Uncle Drayton was already striding across the street, right in front of a pair of oxen hauling a sling-cart, straight toward his daughter.

Austin started off after him. A big, black hand came down on his shoulder.

"Oh no, you don't, Massa Austin," Henry-James said. "You ain't goin' nowhere near them Fire Eaters."

✢ ✤ ✢

Chapter Six

Austin hesitated only a second before he jerked his shoulder away.

"You can't tell me what to do, Henry-James!"

"What you talkin' 'bout, Massa Austin? If'n I *don't* tell you what to do, I's gonna be in a mess of trouble."

"But I want to see what's happening to Kady! Look, Chesnut and Pryor are there now. You can see Chesnut flaring his nostrils from here!"

Henry-James shook his head and kept his hand just an inch from Austin's shoulder.

"I's sorry, Massa Austin, I want to know 'bout Miz Kady, too—"

"Then go with me."

Henry-James shook his head firmly.

"Come on, Henry-James," Charlotte said. "We can hide together in the crowd. Nobody'll even notice Austin."

Henry-James did a little nostril-flaring of his own. "I don't know, Massa Austin."

"Look at that, Henry-James!" Austin cried, pointing frantically.

Roger Pryor, a long-haired, pointy-nosed man, was jerking his head the way he always did, right toward Kady, while short, stout Lawson Chesnut bared his yellow teeth at her. Virgil Rhett grabbed both her arms from behind and jerked them back so that she had to thrust out her chin to keep from slumping forward.

"They're hurting her!" Austin cried.

A low growl came out of Henry-James's throat. Uncle Drayton was still trying to work his way through the parade to the other side of the street. And Lawson Chesnut was tugging at the ribbons on Kady's bonnet with his stubby hands.

"We goin'," Henry-James said. His voice was menacing, and a thrill went up Austin's spine.

With Charlotte on his heels, he plunged after Henry-James, through the crowd on the sidewalk to a spot several yards down where there were no lines of soldiers passing on the street. Henry-James tore across the road with the Ravenal cousins hurrying behind him. On the other side, Henry-James elbowed his way through the throng of people. Normally, the rich planters and their wives and children would have smacked him upside the head without so much as a by-your-leave for shoving in front of white people. But they were all far too wrapped up in the pageantry of the Confederate troops to even notice.

Austin jumped up and down behind Henry-James to try to see. But Henry-James stopped them both at the street lamp and put his arms out.

"What . . . why don't you go over there?" Austin said.

"Marse Drayton, he there now," Henry-James said. "Get you up on this here step, Massa Austin, Miz Lottie—then you can see real good."

There was a small square boxlike ledge around the bottom of the street lamp, and Austin climbed up onto it and held tight to the lamp post so he wouldn't make a fool of himself toppling over into the crowd. They might notice *that*. Charlotte bobbed up easily and held on with one hand.

Just beyond them, Uncle Drayton grabbed stubby Lawson Chesnut by the arm and yanked him away from Kady.

"What do you mean by this, Chesnut!" Uncle Drayton said.

"I am conducting an investigation, Mr. Ravenal," Chesnut said. He tried to sound important, but his voice was wheezing.

He's always been afraid of Uncle Drayton, Austin thought.

"What on earth would you have to investigate my daughter for?" Uncle Drayton said. Once again he smacked Chesnut's hands away from Kady's bonnet and then pulled her forward, out of the clutches of Virgil Rhett.

"Now see here," Rhett cried.

"This young woman is suspected of treason!" Roger Pryor said in his thin, nasal voice. He jerked his head as if to provide an exclamation point.

"Against whom?" Uncle Drayton said.

"The Confederate States of America!" all three Fire Eaters shouted.

Around them, the crowd turned happily from the parade and shouted a response—"The Confederate States of America!"

"You do believe in the Confederacy, do you not, Mr. Ravenal?" Virgil Rhett said. His eyes narrowed suspiciously.

"Not if it gives people the right to search anyone they want to, right on the street!"

"We don't search just anyone," Chesnut wheezed. "Only those we have reason to believe are not on our side."

"My daughter is not—"

"Daddy," Kady said. "I can speak for myself."

Kady's voice was as honey-smooth and clear as ever, and the color was coming back into her cheeks. It occurred to Austin that in that bonnet she looked like a very pretty, honest version of Aunt Olivia. She didn't have the Ravenal pointiness—she was round and soft. And right now she was angry.

"Then speak," Uncle Drayton said. His face looked a little

pinched. "I'll just stand here and make sure these idiots don't try to search your petticoats as well!"

Charlotte clapped her hand over her mouth.

"Mr. Ravenal, I *beg* your pardon!" Chesnut cried. He pulled at his waistcoat and spread his nostrils wide.

"I don't beg yours," Uncle Drayton said. "This entire drama is absolutely indecent. What could you possibly suspect Kady Ravenal—"

"Kady Kearney—that's her name now," Roger Pryor said through his nose.

Chesnut gave his lips a satisfied smack. "That's right, Ravenal. Or didn't you know?"

"I knew," Uncle Drayton said tightly. "Go on."

"Now hold on to your hat, Ravenal," Chesnut said. "This may come as a shock to you—"

"I certainly hope it does!" said Virgil Rhett.

"Oh, for heaven's sake, come out with it!" Kady said. She turned to face her father. "They've accused me of helping runaway slaves get to the North."

It was Austin who clapped his hand over his mouth this time. He felt Charlotte curling her fingers around his sleeve. He was afraid to even look at Henry-James.

"Why, that is preposterous!" Uncle Drayton said.

"Is it?" Chesnut said, gasping for air. "I don't think you would say that if you knew what we know!"

"Which is what?" Kady said. "You still haven't told me."

Chesnut's eyes wavered from her over to Roger Pryor. He jerked his head and glanced at Virgil Rhett, whose eyebrows crawled together again.

"They don't have anything," Austin whispered to Charlotte. "Look at how they're all looking at each other—"

"The dogs!" Roger Pryor suddenly blasted out through his nose.

"What dogs?" Kady said.

Uncle Drayton's face slowly broke into a smile. "Let me be clear on this, gentlemen," he said. "*Dogs* told you that my daughter is assisting maroons in escaping from their masters?"

"They didn't *tell* us," Chesnut said, wheezing mightily.

"They *showed* us!" Rhett said. "The soldiers have special Negro-tracking dogs now that can pick up the scent of one of those wild desperadoes from just a scrap of fabric."

"She passed by the wagon just a while ago, and those animals went mad!" Pryor said. He gave his head three jerks that sent his long hair flying.

Kady threw her head back and laughed so hard that her bonnet fell from her head and hung from her neck by its ribbons.

"That certainly proves it, doesn't it?" she said. "I walk by, smelling like the litter of puppies our dog just slung, and your dogs start barking." She stuck out her hands. "Go ahead, put me in irons. I'll never be able to defend myself against that!"

Rhett moved toward her, but Uncle Drayton pushed him back with an elbow.

"That's all the evidence you have?" Uncle Drayton said.

Austin thought he looked relieved. *He* certainly was. He realized that sweat was pouring from his forehead.

The three men looked at each other.

"For now," Chesnut wheezed at last. He drew his face close to Kady's. "But you watch it, girlie. If they smell anything else on you—"

"There couldn't be anything worse on me than that nasty tobacco breath on you," Kady said.

She smiled at Chesnut and calmly readjusted her bonnet. Chesnut pulled abruptly away and turned to Pryor and Rhett, who stood there, red-faced and stiff.

"Say something!" he barked at them.

But they both shook their heads and looked daggers at Uncle Drayton.

"Now, if there's nothing else, I'd best be on my way," Kady said. She nodded coldly at them. And then she let her eyes rest on her father.

"Good-bye," she said.

"Let me see you home," Uncle Drayton said.

"No, I'll be fine," she said.

She disappeared into the crowd. Austin put one foot down on the ground to go after her, but Henry-James stared him down. Charlotte leaned out from the pole and tried to catch one last glimpse of her. Austin saw the tears shining in her eyes.

"I'm telling you, Ravenal," Lawson Chesnut said, "she's a likely suspect—married to a Yankee like she is."

"He's an Irishman," Uncle Drayton said.

"Well, he's no Southron—and that makes him a suspect in my book!" Pryor cried.

"Then we don't read the same books," said Uncle Drayton.

"Indeed we don't, but I think you'd better start," Chesnut said.

"I thought we agreed that you would no longer threaten me, Mr. Chesnut," Uncle Drayton said. "I am loyal to the South, right or wrong."

"I'm not threatening you, Mr. Ravenal," Chesnut said, "I'm warning you. There's a difference. If you do anything to assist your daughter in any way—should we discover proof that she's part of this Underground Railroad—you'll be a suspect as well."

"We have to do everything we can to stop this, Ravenal, now you know that," Virgil Rhett said.

Austin could see that Uncle Drayton's steely, narrowed eyes were making Rhett nervous.

"Slavery is important to civilized living," Rhett went on. "And every day a runaway slave is free is a reminder to the others that escape is possible."

"We have to make it *im*possible!" Pryor cried nasally. "We have to hunt them relentlessly—"

"And we have to stop this secret escape system!" Chesnut said. "That means putting every person who aids and abets runaway slaves in jail."

"Or running them out of town on the business end of a rifle," Pryor said. "And we don't care if it's a woman!"

"We don't care if it's your *daughter*," Rhett said.

Chesnut stepped in close and poked his stubby finger into Uncle Drayton's chest. "Or you, Mr. Ravenal. If you are not *completely* loyal to this revolution, we'll run you out, too."

Uncle Drayton took hold of Chesnut's finger and threw it away from him. "What revolution?" he said.

"The one we're about to fight!" Pryor cried. He flung an arm toward the parade.

"You're comparing this to the American Revolution?" Uncle Drayton said.

"It's the same thing! We're fighting for our independence for the sake of future generations."

"And your daughter won't have a future, Mr. Ravenal, if we catch her running slaves out of the city of Charleston."

Mr. Pryor seemed to like that statement as his parting words, and he turned smartly on his heel and, of course, jerked his head as he cut out through the crowd. Chesnut wheezed after him. Rhett stayed long enough to give Uncle Drayton one more look at his eyebrows.

"I gots to get you all back across that street 'fore he knows you ever left," Henry-James hissed. "Come on!"

Austin and Charlotte didn't argue with him this time. Austin's head was spinning too fast for him to do anything but follow.

It didn't stop spinning that night as he lay in bed, thinking about Kady and Fitz. When he did fall asleep, it spun on in his dreams, with Kady being chased by dogs and Fitz following with a litter of puppies all breathing nasty tobacco breath. He woke up groping for puppies in his bed. After that, he couldn't go back to sleep.

It wasn't just the fact that the Fire Eaters were now on to Kady, or just that Uncle Drayton was being torn in half by the South he'd always loved so much. It was that everything seemed to be brewing together like the storm Austin now constantly experienced inside himself.

And I can't leave until I do what I'm supposed to do, he thought over and over. *Jesus has me here for a reason still—and I sure wish He'd tell me what it is. I have to fix whatever it is before Father sends for us.*

"Why the long faces, you two?" Polly said the next morning as she sailed gaily with Tot into the garden where Austin and Charlotte were sitting on the joggling board. Its wooden plank seat sagged in unusual stillness. Normally, they'd have been bouncing and giggling for all they were worth.

"No reason," Charlotte said.

"You are such a liar," Polly said.

She settled herself on a garden bench across from them and pointed to the azalea bush behind her. Tot plucked her a flower and handed it to her, then watch open-mouthed as Polly pulled at its petals.

"You look as if someone has died," Polly said. "You both do."

"Somebody might," Austin said. "A lot of people. In case you haven't noticed, they're trying to start a war here."

"Oh, posh!" Polly said. "There isn't going to be any bloodshed! The minute General Beauregard fires on Fort Sumter, those Yankees are going to skeedaddle for their lives and the South will be free—simple as that."

Austin stared at her. Charlotte, too, had her mouth hanging open. Tot just nodded blissfully.

"Where did you hear a bunch of hooey like that?" Austin said.

"It isn't hooey, Boston Austin," Polly said. "You aren't the only one around here with a brain."

"Who else has one?" Charlotte said.

Polly cocked her head slyly over the azalea blossom. "Oh, no one," she said. She pulled off a petal and watched it float to the ground.

Charlotte sat up straight on the board and nudged Austin.

"Now who's the liar?" Charlotte said.

"You didn't let me finish," Polly said. She smiled secretively at Tot. "It's no one *you* know."

"Then how do *you* know him?" Charlotte said.

Austin decided to stay out of this one. It was turning out to be one of those between-sisters arguments that usually ended in nose-pulling.

"Do you think you know everyone I know?" Polly said.

Charlotte nodded.

"Well, you don't. Last night after you *children* were safely tucked into your beds, we adults had visitors."

"Who?" Charlotte said.

"Just a few men from the Citadel," Polly said. She pulled off three more petals, and Charlotte snorted in disgust.

"You watched them from the steps, Polly Ravenal, you know you did!" she said.

Polly dropped the rest of the petals with a satisfied smile. "I did nothing of the kind," she said. "I was invited to join the company in the parlor, and I did. We had tea and cakes and talked about the war. Corporal Wylie said for me not to worry my pretty head about any fighting." She tossed her thin curls. "I've told you the rest."

"I wish Kady were here," Charlotte said fiercely.

"Why?" Polly said. "So she could try to steal him away from me? She wouldn't get far. Corporal Wylie told me he would never be interested in a girl who didn't support the Confederacy with all her heart and soul."

"So now you do?" Charlotte said. "If Kady were here, she'd tell me this whole thing was something you made up."

Polly sniffed lightly and stood up. Tot lunged toward her to gather up her morning skirt so it wouldn't drag on the ground. As usual, she exposed several inches of pantalettes in the process.

"Think what you want," Polly said airily. "People who are jealous often think the worst of others."

She floated out with Tot clutching madly at the skirts. Charlotte watched her go, her own face red as a newly cooked beet.

"She is *such* a liar!" she said.

"I don't know," Austin said. "I think she might have been telling the truth."

"And just what do you know about it, Austin Hutchinson? Have you read about *courting*, too?" She was puffing up and going crimson.

"I did read some in a ladies' magazine my mother had, but—"

"You can't read about things like that in a book," Charlotte said.

"How do you find out about it, then?" he said.

She shrugged and sagged, deflated. "I don't know. I guess you just have to grow up to be a man or a woman, and then you just know it, don't you think?"

That made Austin feel uneasy. The word *man* was having that effect on him these days.

Charlotte slumped back down on the joggling board and sighed.

"What's wrong?" Austin said.

"What Polly said—about Kady not believing in the

Confederacy. That's what those men said last night. Have you thought about it?"

"That's *all* I can think about," Austin said.

"And now even Daddy can't defend her."

Austin grunted.

"What does that mean?" Charlotte said.

"I'd sure defend her. Matter of fact, if they try to do anything to her, I *will*!"

"And just how you think you gonna do that, Massa Austin?"

Henry-James ambled across the garden, a pair of Uncle Drayton's boots and a rag in his hands.

"I don't know," Austin said. "I'd think of something. I always do."

"Thinkin' ain't the same as fightin'," Henry-James said. He settled himself on a garden rock and spit on the toe of one of the boots. "If'n you gonna fight the likes of them Fire Eatin' people, you gots to do more than read about it in books."

"I *know*!" Austin said. His shoulder blades started to pinch. "I don't read books *all* the time."

"Those are grown-up men, though, Austin," Charlotte said. "Nobody our age could fight them—except maybe Henry-James." She added hurriedly, "And he's older, anyway."

"I don't think about how old I am or anything!" Austin said. "If Kady needs help, I'm going to be there!"

"Uh-huh," Henry-James said.

He went on shining. Charlotte and Austin fell into a sullen silence.

Here we go again, Austin thought. *The old Austin-is-just-a-puffball-like-his-father spiel. I'm getting sick of this!*

"What's this now?"

They both looked up to see Uncle Drayton in a pearl-gray morning coat.

"You two aren't at each other's throats like everyone else, are you?" he said.

He stood in front of them and folded his arms as he watched them. Charlotte squirmed uncomfortably on the joggling board. Austin just shrugged.

"I won't have this—not for a minute," Uncle Drayton said. "The rest of us can squabble all we want—we're a bunch of stubborn old things anyway. But when the two of you take to fighting, now that's worse than this Civil War they're talking about."

Uncle Drayton's eyes were twinkling in that charming way he had, but his mouth was serious. Austin glanced at Charlotte to see if she saw it, too. She was hanging her head and studying her hands.

"I tell you what," Uncle Drayton said. "Henry-James."

Henry-James lifted his gaze from the boots.

"Yessir," he said in his soft servant's voice.

"Take these children on a picnic. Take Tot and Polly, too. I'll have Josephine pack a basket. Go on down to the waterfront—play some games. I don't want to see any more sour, sad faces than I have to."

"Yessir," Henry-James said.

Austin felt himself brighten a little. Charlotte, too, looked up and gave a half smile.

"I want to see big grins and bright eyes when you return," Uncle Drayton said.

But the eyes he directed at Henry-James were stern. He said, "And you remember, boy—you are responsible for these children."

He looked at Austin and Charlotte again and reached out and touched Charlotte softly on the head. "This mess adults have made," he said, "should never affect my daughters—never in a million years. I hate that most of all."

With another smile, he strode off toward the house.

‡ ‑❖‑ ‡

Chapter Seven

They all had to admit it was a good idea, even Polly. Of course, Polly was in such a pleasant frame of mind, Austin decided she'd have thought snipping off an earlobe was a good idea. She rode inside the smallest of the family carriages with Charlotte and Tot as if she were going coaching with Beauregard himself. Charlotte rolled her eyes at Austin as he shut the door for them.

Austin rode up in the driver's seat with Henry-James and swiveled his head from side to side the way he always did when they rode around in Charleston. There was so much to see that he never noticed the same thing twice.

The city was a bundle of nerves now, which made it all the more exciting. Newspaper boys held stacks of papers and shouted, "When will the war begin? Read all about it here!" Clumps of men stood on street corners, talking until their faces turned red and waving their arms. Young women dashed around in their secession bonnets, chattering to each other—and secretly making eyes at all the young men who were flaunting their uniforms. Austin was sure that inside the coach, Polly must be drooling by now.

But Uncle Drayton had been right—it was much more peaceful down on the waterfront, on the Cooper River side of the

Charleston Peninsula. The residents there, the birds and the fish, seemed unaware that the South was on the brink of war with its northern neighbors over that silly fort that stood hulking on an island out in the harbor. Once the carriage passed the Customs House with its great columns and flurry of merchants, it was as if there were no such thing as war.

"Look, Henry-James!" Austin called out. "That's a pelican!"

"Yessir, it is," Henry-James said calmly.

Austin shrieked as the bird with the hunched-over neck smacked the water headfirst.

"Now that bird there is a white heron," he said, pointing to a skinny-legged bird that was picking its way along the shore. "And that's a tern. I've never seen one in person—only in books."

He went on to rattle off a commentary on the osprey, egrets, cormorants, and the several varieties of seagull he spotted. Henry-James nodded and uttered uh-huhs through it all as he guided the carriage down a little slope that led almost to the narrow sandy beach.

Austin stood up and craned his neck to look at the water. Waves were rolling, softly, one on top of another, tipped in snowy peaks and veined with white foam. A duck rode one in, bobbing happily on the surface, his head high.

"I want to do that!" Austin said.

"You ain't gonna do nothin' of the kind, Massa Austin—'less you wants me to be sold on down the road to Georgia."

"Oh, look at that!" Austin nearly toppled off the carriage as he pointed farther out into the water, where a gray fin was weaving up and down as if it were sewing. "That's got to be a porpoise!" he cried.

He jumped off the driver's seat and hit the ground running. He could hear Charlotte squealing behind him as he raced across the sand to the water's edge.

"It is a porpoise!" he shouted to her. "Look at him jump!"

"There are two—no, three!"

It was as if they were putting on a show just for the cousins. They cut through the water with their fins, then leaped up and splashed back down, crinkling the surface like tinfoil with the sun on it.

"They're so lucky," Charlotte said. "They get to swim in cider."

"Cider?" Austin said.

"Doesn't it look like cider to you—the color and all that foam?"

"I have to taste it," Austin said.

With another squeal from Charlotte, he skidded to his knees. A wave splashed softly in front of him, and he cupped his hands in and scooped up two palms full of water. The minute it hit his lips, he spewed it back out, laughing. It tasted nothing like cider.

"Oh, Austin, how disgusting!" Polly said behind him. "All those ducks and birds dipping in and out of there—and you're *drinking* it?"

"Look, another pelican!" Austin froze and watched as the comical bird skimmed the surface of the water, first flapping his wings, then straightening them to glide easily, then flapping again.

"I don't know whether I'd rather swim or fly," he said. "Look how high up that gull is. He looks like he's inked onto the sky."

"I'd rather eat, if'n it was me," Henry-James said.

He produced the picnic basket that Josephine had filled to overflowing.

"All right," Austin said. "Let's get this over with so we can have some fun!"

"A gentleman never rushes a meal," Polly said. She wafted a hand out for Tot to spread a blanket on the sand.

"That doesn't make any difference to me," Austin said. "I wasn't planning on being a gentleman."

Polly looked at him in horror.

"Well, I mean, I'll be nice to people and all that, but that isn't *all* I'm going to be." He took the basket from Henry-James, peered into it, and started an inventory. "Fresh strawberry preserves. Hickory cured ham. Cornbread. Clabber. Peppermint cakes. Deviled oysters."

"Don't stand there talking about it," Polly said. "Let's eat it."

Austin grinned. Good. He'd steered her away from that conversation. The next step was sure to be some remark about his manhood.

Tot unpacked the basket, which resulted in some cornbread spilling on the blanket and one oyster falling into the sand.

"That's all right," Charlotte told her. "You'll make one of those gulls happy."

Even as she spoke, a smoky-gray gull was stalled above them, eyeing the treasure and crying.

Austin took a bite out of a ham biscuit and leaned back to survey the sky. It was a brilliant blue, with some clouds dotted here and there—big ones that were gray in the center with white fringe around the edges. Just beyond them, a long pier reached out into the water over a small island beneath it that stood out in the harbor like a thick, green rug. The lower parts of the pier's posts were covered with barnacles and oysters that clung to them in flowery bunches. Austin passed up a deviled oyster in honor of them.

"Food tastes better when you eat it outside, by the water," he said.

"You're talking with your mouth full," Polly said. "A gentleman doesn't do that."

"Woffa woffa schmay, falla?" Charlotte said.

Austin grinned at her. She was talking away, her mouth stuffed to capacity with cornbread.

"Very funny," Polly said.

I thought so, Austin told himself. He rested on his elbows and stretched his legs off the blanket and onto the sand. The sun bathed his face. Heaven, he decided, must be a lot like this.

"We should play something really special when we're finished eating," he said. "Something to mark the day."

"I have an announcement to make," Polly said.

"Corporal Wylie proposed," Charlotte said.

"No," Polly said, visibly controlling her mouth. "I just want you all to know that I no longer play."

"Why not?" Austin said.

"Because I am officially a lady now."

Charlotte glared over a peppermint cake. "Who says?"

"No one had to *say*. I just know that when a girl begins to get attention from a young man, she is no longer a child."

"You've been getting attention for a long time from young men," Austin said. "Every time you drop your handkerchief, one of them picks it up."

Tot nodded thoughtfully. Polly gave her a smoldering look. "I am talking about attention that is *his* idea. There was no handkerchief dropping with Corporal Wylie. He spoke to me first."

"Did he, Tot?" Charlotte said.

Tot's eyes went wild.

"I'm tired of talking about this," Austin said. "Let's play something—those of us who still play."

"Tot and I will keep watch over the picnic things," Polly said. She tightened the scarf that held her hat in place. "You children go on and have your fun."

"Oh, brother," Charlotte said to Austin as the two of them and Henry-James walked on down the beach. "She certainly is putting on airs now, isn't she? That Corporal Wylie person probably doesn't even remember her name today."

"He probably didn't know it last night, if the truth's known," Austin said.

Henry-James cleared his throat. "Yessir, he did, Massa Austin. I was right there, servin' up them spice cakes. That there Corporal Wylie, he knowed her name sure 'nuff."

"That's because Daddy is so polite, he makes sure everyone is introduced—"

"Let's *play*," Austin said.

"You name the game, Massa Austin."

Austin looked out over the harbor and watched a sailing craft sitting still, almost lifeless, on the water. There wasn't a breath of air stirring. It was almost eerie.

"Pirates," he said. "Like Steve Bonet and his buccaneers."

"I'll be a buccaneer!" Charlotte said.

"He had 29 of them. They were all hanged from the same tree down on the Battery."

"I won't be a buccaneer," she said quickly. "I know how realistic you get when you play, Austin."

"You tell me what one of them buccaneers is, and I'll be one," Henry-James said. "Long as I don't got to hang from no tree."

"I have a better idea," Austin said. "Let's pretend we're black seamen of today."

"We all gonna be black?" Henry-James said. "How come?"

"Because whenever a ship comes into a port in South Carolina, if the ship is going to stay for any length of time, they lock all the black seamen up in prison while it's here. I read that."

"Are they criminals?" Charlotte said.

"No, they're just black."

"That's horrible!"

"I know—so let's pretend we've escaped from the prison to an island."

"Where we gonna find an island?" Henry-James said.

Austin pointed out to the pier. "Right there. It's not that far out. We could wade to it."

"We ain't goin' in no water," Henry-James said. He narrowed

his eyes into slits at Austin. "Ain't a one of us can swim—we almost drowned a couple times before."

"He's right," Charlotte said. "I don't think we should—"

"Then we can climb down from the pier!" Austin said.

"What you talkin' 'bout, Massa Austin?" Henry-James said.

"Well, look. See how that one post goes right down beside the island? We can climb up and down tree trunks. Why can't we shinny down that?"

"Um—" Charlotte stopped.

" 'Um' what?" Austin said.

She looked helplessly at Henry-James.

"Me and Miz Lottie could, Massa Austin," Henry-James said. "We don't know 'bout you."

Austin's shoulder blades squeezed together. "I'm not some little weakling!" he said.

"I knows that," Henry-James said. "But that there post—"

"Is easy as pie," Austin said. "Now do you all want to play or not?"

"I want to play," Charlotte said. She watched herself draw a circle in the sand with her toe. Her hair lifted off her shoulders in the breeze. "But why don't we pick another game?"

"Just because you don't think I can climb down that post? That's silly!"

She didn't make a move and neither did Henry-James. He just looked out over the harbor as if he were waiting for his ship to come in. Charlotte dug deeper with her toe. Austin wanted to scream.

I'm not a little sissy! I can do things! I'm not just a bookworm like my father! Why can't you see that?

He stopped as if a bolt of lightning had just struck him. Was that the reason God wanted him to stay here? Was that the thing he was supposed to finish up before he left? Assure them that he was strong enough and tough enough and manly enough to take on the world if he had to? That *that* was the person Jesus wanted him to be?

The thought whirled in his mind, even as some sand kicked up in a flurry of breeze around his feet. That was it. That had to be it. And there was no time like now to show them.

"It's a great game," he said. "And I'm going to play it—with you or without you."

Not waiting for an answer, he marched off down the beach toward the pier. In a moment, Charlotte was beside him, and he could feel Henry-James right on his heels.

"There're barnacles all over those posts," Charlotte said.

"Oysters, too," Henry-James put in.

"I know," Austin said. "But only where the water touches. If we climb down the dry part, that'll get us low enough to drop right down onto the island."

"Oh," Charlotte said.

She didn't argue any more as they reached the entrance to the pier and started their way down its gray, creaky boards toward the island. There were flags at the other end, one for South Carolina, one for the new Confederacy—the "Stars and Bars" they were calling it. Austin could hear their thick ropes slapping against their poles.

"It's getting windier," Charlotte said.

"That just makes it more exciting," Austin said.

"I'm not excited about my skirts flying up over my head," she said.

She plastered her arms at her sides to hold her dress down and once again looked at Henry-James. Austin didn't wait for Henry-James's answer. He trotted on down the pier and leaned over the railing to look down at the island.

It actually looked farther down than it had appeared from the beach. Even from the top of the wet part of the post, it was going to be a long drop.

But there was no way he was going to admit that now. Not with Henry-James grunting behind him.

Charlotte joined him at the railing and took a look.

"Just like going down a tree," Austin said before she could say anything. "You have to admit I can climb trees much better than I could when I came here."

"Of course you can," Charlotte said. "You'd never even climbed one before. How could you get any worse?"

Austin hitched his shoulders up.

"I didn't mean to sound ugly," she said.

"Doesn't bother me," Austin said. "All right, are we escaped black seamen or not?"

"That's gonna take some pretty tall pretendin', Massa Austin," Henry-James said. " 'Cause you ain't black and you ain't from the sea and you sure ain't—"

"Don't say it, Henry-James!" Austin shouted at him. "Don't you dare say I'm not a man!"

"Hold on, Massa Austin—"

"Just hush up, all right? Just shut yourself right up!"

If there had been a storm in Austin before, there was a *tornado* going on now. Getting down on his hands and knees, he ducked his head down to see under the pier. There was a brace securing the post and forming a triangle. He stuck one foot down onto it, still holding on to the pier, and then put his other one down there, too. Inching quickly, he wrapped his arms around the part of the pole that rose above the pier, so that he was half above it and half below it. He would have liked to have taken a little more time to plan how he was going to proceed, but to go slow would have looked like he was scared. And he was too mad— and had too much to prove—to act afraid.

"Massa Austin, I don' know 'bout this," Henry-James said. "I'm s'pose to be keepin' a eye on you."

"Then I guess you'd better climb down here with me," Austin said.

He bent his knees and lowered one hand below the other until he was all the way under the pier.

"All right, Massa Austin," Henry-James said. "But not today. We got us a *big* wind kickin' up."

Austin glanced out over the harbor. The sailing craft was leaning now, almost as if it were going to fall over. Even as he looked, a strong breeze scooted along the pier and set his loose shirt to flapping against his back.

"That's right, Austin," Charlotte called down. "Even the seamen wouldn't chance it in a storm."

"There isn't going to be a storm," Austin said. "It's a beautiful day!"

"You can't see them clouds?" Henry-James said. "They's started to blow theyselves right in a line."

Austin looked up. In the short time since he'd watched their fringe drift peacefully above him, they'd turned to an annoyed-looking gray and had formed a wall like the Battery itself—a moving wall that scudded along the sky.

Just then, he felt something wet at his ankles. He looked down and saw the water leaping up like tongues toward his feet. Another breeze—a real wind this time—lashed against the pier and sent the water up again. It splashed onto the back of Austin's cotton trousers and plastered him to the pole.

The top of the pole was at once as slippery as the sweat that was forming in Austin's palms. He tried to cling to it with his knees, but both legs slid down the slick wood.

He was left hanging by his fingers from the brace, feet dangling in the rising wind.

✧✦✧

Chapter Eight

"Austin!" Charlotte screamed.

Her face appeared just below the pier, eyes wide, hair streaming out like seaweed.

Austin squeezed his fingers around the brace. "I'm falling!"

"Hold on with your knees!"

"I can't! It's too slippery!"

"Get out the way, Miz Lottie!" he heard Henry-James shout.

All of a sudden, the whole world seemed noisy. There were gulls screaming and wind wailing and water pounding. What a short time before had been an eerie stillness was now a full-fledged gale—and it was blowing Austin's body like one of the flags.

Charlotte's face disappeared, and Henry-James's took its place. He thrust down a strong black arm.

"Grab hold!" he shouted.

Austin wanted to. There was no pretending to be a real man now. But try as he might, he couldn't get his fingers to uncurl from the brace. They stayed there, trembling and white-knuckled.

"This ain't no time for pretend, Massa Austin!" Henry-James screamed at him. "Grab hold my arm!"

"I can't," Austin cried. "I can't let go!"

"Yes, you can, Austin!" Charlotte called out from somewhere above him. "Henry-James won't let you fall!"

"You know I won't, Massa Austin!" Henry-James said. "Come on now—catch hold!"

Once again, Austin tried to get his fingers to unfold from the brace. But the water was coming up high, slamming his knees and shins into the pole. If he let go with one hand—what if he fell before Henry-James could grab him? He'd drown—or be cut to death by barnacles before he ever got to the water.

He looked down. The green island had disappeared under the churning of the angry gray water. A glance over the other shoulder showed the sailboat tossing and pitching like a toy on the harbor. If the storm could do that to a boat, what chance did he have?

"What are you doing?" he heard Charlotte cry out.

Henry-James didn't answer. He just thrust the upper part of his body under the railing and held it straight out over the water. Stretching down, he could touch Austin's fingers.

"I'm right here, Massa Austin! Just turn loose, and I got you!"

"Are you sure?"

"Just grab hold!"

Austin squeezed his eyes shut.

"Come on, Austin! You can do it! You're brave!"

"No, I'm scared! I'm scared I'll fall!"

"I ain't gonna let you fall, Massa. Come on now!"

But Henry-James didn't wait for Austin to let go of the brace. He pried his fingers loose with his hand and grabbed on to them. Austin at once squeezed until he could feel his fingernails digging into Henry-James's flesh.

Henry-James quickly got a firm hold on Austin's forearm with both hands.

"Now you gots to let go with the other hand," he called out.

"And you gots to hurry 'cause this here water is risin'!"

Austin nodded.

"So do it!" Charlotte cried. "Hurry, Austin!"

Austin nodded again, and he tried, but his fingers remained. He kicked in terror.

"No, don't do that, Massa Austin!" Henry-James shouted. "You gots to be still and let go with the other hand!"

"I'll help!" Charlotte shouted.

Austin looked up and saw her down on her stomach, sliding so far out that Austin didn't see how she was staying on the pier. Her hair was pasted to the sides of her head now, and for the first time Austin realized it was raining in sheets. Still, he couldn't let go. Even when he could feel her wet hand on his fingers, he couldn't let go, and by now his arms were aching, and only the fear was keeping him from dropping like a soaked sponge into the water below.

I'm going to die here, he thought wildly. *I'm going to hang here for the rest of my life, and then I'm going to die.*

But he didn't die. His hand only gave way and dropped limply from the brace. Just as it went, Charlotte grabbed on.

"Hold still, Austin!" she screamed at him. "I've got you!"

For a second, he thought she did. Her skin groped against his and he tried to grab and so did she.

And then there was a scream, and a tangle of petticoats and pantalettes dropped past him.

"Miz Lottie!" Henry-James screamed.

With a painful wrench, he yanked Austin up by his one arm until his chin grazed the pier. Pulling hand over hand, he hauled him onto the boards only enough to get his stomach out of the air.

Austin twisted himself over in time to see Henry-James disappear under the pier.

"No!" Austin cried. "You'll drown!"

But Henry-James wasn't swimming. As Austin scrambled for the side, he saw Henry-James swing from the brace like a trapeze artist and slide down the pole. He simply hung on and slid until he hit the water.

"There're barnacles!" Austin shouted crazily. He stared, stricken, into the water Henry-James had just disappeared into. *Why didn't I think of that before I started this whole stupid thing?*

Wriggling out as far as he could, he searched the water with horrified eyes. At first there was nothing but madly swirling eddies of foam. They were drowning, both of them. They couldn't swim, and he knew they were being washed away in the storm.

I threw them into it! I'm so stupid!

But just as he was considering hurling himself in with them, a head bobbed up, a black kinky-haired one that stood up strong against the wind.

"Henry-James!" Austin shouted. "Are you alive?"

It may have been his stupidest question yet, he knew, but it was all he could say.

Henry-James then lifted something up out of the water and slung it over his shoulder.

"Charlotte!" Austin cried.

Henry-James began to move toward the shore. Austin inched down the pier on his stomach, still shouting.

"What are you doing, Henry-James? You can't swim!"

But Henry-James was walking—heavily, as if he were moving through iron. Austin had been right about only one thing. They could have waded out to the island.

Getting himself up from the boards, Austin took off, slipping and sliding, down the pier. At the beach end, he jumped the railing, toppled into the drenched sand and flailed out into the water to meet them.

"Is she alive?" he shouted to Henry-James.

There was no need to ask, however. Charlotte was squawking like a caught chicken and clawing at Henry-James's chest and kicking her feet.

Henry-James didn't even look at Austin, and he ignored Charlotte's protests to put her down. He just made his way through the driving rain with the girl on his shoulder and his jaw stretched out in the lead.

"She's all right, isn't she?" Austin shouted. "Isn't she all right?"

But it was apparent that she wasn't. Tripping along beside them with his heart pounding, Austin could see blood flowing on Charlotte's arms. There was even some in her hair and more seeping out through her stockings.

Dear God, Austin cried inside, *please don't let her bleed to death. Please!*

And then another thought came to him. *You should have talked to God a lot sooner, Austin. You should have asked Him and then this never would have happened.*

"Charlotte Ravenal, what on *earth*!"

Polly was hurrying toward them, holding up her own skirts from the mud while Tot ran along behind her trying to keep the blanket over Polly's head. Austin was surprised Polly even came out in the rain. When she got closer, he could see that her face was pinched and white.

"What happened? Henry-James, what have you allowed to happen to my sister?"

"I'm all right!" Charlotte shouted over the wind. "Please put me down, Henry-James!"

"No'm, I'm gettin' you to the carriage, and I'm takin' you home!"

With that, he charged off through the storm toward the carriage at a trot so fast that Austin could barely keep up. Polly pushed at Tot.

"Go put that blanket over Charlotte before she catches her death of pneumonia."

Pneumonia!

Austin's mother had had pneumonia more than once. People could *die* from that. Daddy Elias had.

Polly took hold of Austin's arm. He was so defeated that he didn't even pull away.

"What happened, Austin?" she said.

"It's my fault," he muttered.

But she didn't hear him. She was already barking orders at Tot on how to wrap Charlotte in the blanket.

"You ride up with Henry-James, Austin," Polly said. "She needs the room to lie down."

Austin climbed miserably up on the driver's seat. Henry-James was already there, stiffly holding the reins and staring straight ahead. Rain spilled over his face.

He didn't say a word as he guided the carriage through the rutted slurries of mud the streets had become. It could get stuck up to the hubs if he wasn't careful, and there would be no help for it if he broke a wheel or an axle in a pothole. It took all of Henry-James's concentration.

But Austin knew that wasn't the only reason he wasn't talking. He had never seen Henry-James's jaw locked so tight, or seen his eyes drawn into such narrow, livid slits. Austin was *afraid* for him to speak. He sat huddled on the seat, letting the rain pelt him in the face. In spite of how angry Uncle Drayton was going to be with him when he found out what Austin had done, he wished from the pit of his stomach that he had been the one to take that fall instead of Charlotte.

It wasn't until Henry-James turned the carriage around the point toward the East Battery and a corner streetlight shone on him that Austin saw the blood trailing down his slave friend's arm.

"You're hurt!" Austin said.

Henry-James didn't answer.

"What am I saying? Of course you are! You slid down that pole, all covered with barnacles and oysters, just like you told me. I should have listened to you, Henry-James! I'm so sorry—"

"What's done's done," Henry-James said.

There wasn't a trace of forgiveness in his eyes.

"I'll never do anything like that again," Austin said. "I promise. You both could have been killed."

He didn't answer.

"Please, Henry-James. I know I was wrong. I don't blame you for being mad at me, but . . ."

There was no point in going on. Henry-James kept his face like a stone, even as they pulled into the drive at the big townhouse on the East Battery. It was agony for Austin.

His heart didn't even lift when he opened the carriage door and Charlotte was sitting up chewing Polly out.

"Stop wrapping this blanket around me, Polly!" she said. "I feel like one of those Egyptian mummies. I'm all right. I just got a little water in me is all."

"Oh, and that would be why you're bleeding," Polly said, giving her very wet non-curls a flip.

"I'm not bleeding—that's Henry-James's blood! He's the one you should be fussing over."

But nobody could fuss like Aunt Olivia, who started the moment Henry-James carried Charlotte in the side door to the sitting room, where she had been napping while Mousie fanned her.

"My precious baby!" she shrieked. "What happened, my lamb? A carriage accident?" She turned on Henry-James. "You wretched cuffee! Why weren't you paying attention to what you were doing? She could be dying!"

"It wasn't a carriage accident, Mama," Polly said. "And she's not dying."

"With blood from head to toe? How can you even say such a thing? Why didn't we bring Ria? Sally doesn't need her!"

"Put her on the sofa, Henry-James," Polly said. "Tot, go fetch a pan of water and some clean rags. You boys will have to leave the room while we dress her wounds."

"I don't *have* any wounds!" Charlotte said. She settled unhappily on the sofa and folded her arms with a scowl.

"I'll be the judge of that," Polly said. "Mama, sit down. You look pale. Mousie, see to her. Get the spirits of ammonia."

Aunt Olivia blinked at her for a moment, and then sagged against Mousie, as if looking pale weren't such a bad idea. Polly shooed a hand at Austin and Henry-James.

"Go on, now. This is no place for males."

Austin looked warily at Charlotte, but she grinned at him and shook her head. He felt a ripple of relief. It was her "I'll talk to *you* later" look.

He turned to follow Henry-James out of the room, when the door came open and Uncle Drayton's tall shadow fell across them. His eyes went at once to Charlotte, and they flickered open in alarm.

"Don't worry, Daddy," Polly said. She was pulling Charlotte's hair gently away from her face and studying her forehead where there was a smear of blood.

Uncle Drayton flew across the room shouting, "Mousie, fetch a doctor!"

"No, Daddy, I'm fine. This is Henry-James's blood. He rescued me!"

Austin could see Charlotte's face and the back of Uncle Drayton's head. Charlotte broke into a smile, and her eyes danced at her father. And then as if she'd been slapped, her glow faded, and Austin saw her mouth start a slow pucker. Uncle Drayton's neck stiffened like a pole.

"Daddy—what?" Charlotte said.

Uncle Drayton pulled away from her and slowly stood up, as if he were gathering himself, gathering his thoughts. When he turned around, his eyes were smoldering as they sought out the source of his anger.

Austin looked, too. The fearsome gaze fell right on Henry-James.

"Boy," Uncle Drayton said, "what has happened to my little girl?"

Austin swallowed. "I think you better let me tell it, Uncle Drayton. I was the one who—"

"Quiet," Uncle Drayton said. He didn't take his eyes off Henry-James. "I want to hear it from him. Speak!"

Austin looked helplessly around the room. There was no ally there—no Kady, no Mother, no Daddy Elias. There wasn't even a Jefferson to scream out the facts before anybody could stop him.

I can scream them! Austin thought. *Somebody has to!*

"I was making them play a game with me," Austin cried. "I climbed down from the pier and got stuck and Henry-James was trying to save me when—"

"I said quiet!"

The words roared out of Uncle Drayton and rattled Austin into silence. Still Uncle Drayton bored his eyes into Henry-James, as he took a long step toward him and took him roughly by the shoulder.

"Come with me," he said.

"Daddy, what are you going to do?"

Charlotte came up off the sofa, shaking Polly's hand off her arm.

"I am going to take my slave where I can deal with him without being told my business. Stay here—all of you!"

The door had slammed behind them before Austin could uproot himself from the floor. By the time he got out into the hall, Uncle Drayton was headed up the elegant curved staircase as if it were a prison walkway, dragging Henry-James by the back of his neck and talking through his teeth.

"Uncle Drayton, let me *explain*!" Austin called after him.

His uncle stopped just as he was about to disappear around the curve. Austin took a huge breath.

"There's no need to punish Henry-James. It wasn't his fault—it was mine! Charlotte was trying to rescue me and she fell and he saved her life. We both could have drowned if it hadn't been for him. He was doing what you told him—he was protecting us."

For a long moment, Uncle Drayton looked at him, as if his mind-wheels were spinning in the mud. In that long moment, Austin dared to hope he'd gotten through. He chanced just one more sentence.

"I was trying to prove something—"

"What?"

Austin stopped. If it had been for anyone else but Henry-James, he would never tell such a pathetic thing about himself. His cheeks started to burn.

"I was trying to show that I'm not just like my father. I'm not a—"

"Austin, you are *exactly* like your father," Uncle Drayton said. "I've told you that. And this time, my boy, that is not a good thing to be."

He gritted his teeth and gave Henry-James a shake by the back of his neck. "You Hutchinsons would stand up for a slave if he murdered your mother. And I have had enough of it. I tell you, I have had enough."

Then burying his fingers into the flesh of Henry-James's arms, he shoved him up the stairs.

✝–✦–✝

Chapter Nine

ustin followed them, but Uncle Drayton's anger gave the man speed. He had locked and bolted the attic door by the time Austin reached the third floor. No amount of banging and begging convinced him to open it.

In fact, he finally shouted, "Austin, if you do not go away, I will beat this boy to within an inch of his life."

"Are you going to do that anyway—for something he didn't even do?"

"No! Now leave—or I shall!"

Austin leaned against the door for a long time, but Uncle Drayton was true to his word. There was no sound of a whip or a cat-o'-nine-tails. There wasn't even any shouting. When he heard his uncle coming, he ducked into the darkness of a dormer window and crouched there as Uncle Drayton came out and locked the door behind him with a key.

When Austin was certain he was gone, he crawled to the door and tried to peer through the keyhole. It was too dark to see anything.

"Henry-James," he whispered.

There was no answer.

Of course not. He'll probably never speak to me again now.

But Austin had to talk to *him*. He stood for a moment in the darkness and tried to think. The key. He had to get the key.

The answer was so easy that he almost didn't believe it could work. Not waiting to second-guess himself, Austin hurried down the stairs and into the long, windowed hallway that ran across the back of the house. He wasn't sure which of the little rooms Mousie stayed in when she wasn't waiting on Aunt Olivia, but since she and Josephine were the only ones staying in the slaves' quarters right now, she shouldn't be hard to find.

A tap on the second door brought a tiny voice to the crack.

"Who there?" she whispered.

"It's me, Mousie," he said. "I need to talk to you."

It really didn't take much talking to get to the key basket Mousie kept in her care. She was always driven to momentary stupidity by Austin's long strings of conversation.

"I hope you don't mind, but I'm locked out and I don't want to disturb Aunt Olivia, her being all hysterical over Charlotte and all. High-strung, isn't she? Oh, there's the basket—I'll just help myself if you don't mind." He crossed to the one chair in the room where the basket was sitting and saw with relief that each key had an identifying tag attached to it with a ribbon.

"Save you the trouble," he rattled on. "You work so hard, Mousie. And you never complain, not even a peep. You're a martyr is all—a Christian martyr."

Mousie was still blinking when he left the room with the key. As he hurried off down the hall, he was sure he heard just one little squeak.

Everyone seemed to be sulking in his or her room as Austin took the steps two at a time up to the attic. He prayed all the way.

Please, please, let Henry-James forgive me.

He couldn't even think about what he would do if his prayers weren't answered. He only wished he'd started praying before he'd decided to prove what a man he was.

I'll be anything You want me to be, he prayed as he jiggled the key in the attic door lock. *Even a puffball weakling.*

It was so dark and soundless inside the attic that he thought for a moment Henry-James had somehow gotten away. But as his eyes grew accustomed to the lack of light, he saw his friend's dark form in the corner farthest from the one narrow window.

"It's me, Henry-James," Austin whispered.

There was no answer. He expected that. What he didn't expect was what he found when he had fumbled his way to the corner.

Henry-James was chained to the wall.

"No! Henry-James, no! He can't do this to you!"

Henry-James didn't look up. He kept his eyes riveted to the floor.

"Looks like he done it," he said.

"I'm cutting you loose," Austin said.

He looked around frantically for something sharp. Beside him, he heard Henry-James give a hard laugh.

"It isn't funny. I have to do something!"

"What you gonna do, Massa Austin? 'Scuse me for sayin', but ain't you done enough already?"

Austin dropped to his knees in front of Henry-James, where he couldn't help but look at him.

"I know it's my fault! You heard me try to tell Uncle Drayton that."

"He don't care none 'bout whose fault it is," Henry-James said.

Austin nodded miserably. "I heard that, too. That's why I have to get this chain off you."

"And what gonna happen next time Marse Drayton come up here and I'm dancin' 'round this here attic like a free man?"

"I don't know. I'll think of something." But he sank down onto his knees and stared hard at the floor. "I always do, don't I? And it always gets us in trouble."

There was a long silence. Austin fought back a lump in his throat the size of a squirrel.

Please don't let him hate me. Please, I have to help him. I'll be anything You want.

"Not always."

Austin looked up sharply. Henry-James was still staring at the floor, but his mouth had loosened from its line.

"You don't always get us in trouble, Massa Austin. Sometimes you gets us out."

"Is that true?" Austin said. He felt like a puppy, begging for a pat on the head.

"I reckon it is. But this time you can't do nothin', and I sure 'nuff wish you could. I can't take this, Massa Austin. This one thing I can't take at all."

Austin looked at the chain that ran from its hook on the wall to the heavy metal collar around Henry-James's neck. There was still blood blotched on Henry-James's skin and clothes from where he had cut himself rescuing Charlotte. Austin had to force himself not to turn away and retch on the floor.

"Daddy 'Lias, he done tol' me bein' a slave, that what the Lord done made us and that what we got to settle for best we can." Henry-James shook his head at the chain. "But Daddy 'Lias didn't never get chained up like no animal. He always a man. Long as he could be a man, he could be a slave."

Henry-James didn't go on. Austin looked away to give him a chance to swallow his tears.

Please, no matter what I did today—or yesterday—please help me.

"One thing I learn from Daddy 'Lias that I ain't never gonna forget," Henry-James said suddenly.

"What's that?"

"He say when you feel called in spirit, you got to do something 'bout it, no matter what."

"What's that mean—'called in spirit'?"

"That's when you knows real strong you wants to do some-thing—and you can't even say 'zactly why. It maybe don't even make no sense, but you got you a plan, and you knows that what you got to do."

Austin liked the sound of that. "Do you feel 'called in spirit'?"

"I does. Sittin' here chained to the wall like a wild thing, I knows what I gots to do. Trouble is, it go right against what Daddy 'Lias done tol' me to do."

Austin watched his friend's eyes glittering in the darkness.

"You want to run away, don't you, Henry-James?" he said.

Slowly, Henry-James nodded.

The words hung over them as if they were giving Henry-James a chance to take them back. He didn't.

"All right," Austin said. "Then I'm going to help you."

"Only one thing you could do, Massa Austin," Henry-James said.

"Anything. I'll do anything."

"I needs for you to go to Miz Kady and tell her I'm ready. She done tol' me anytime—"

"I'm halfway there already!" Austin whispered.

He scrambled up from his knees, but Henry-James caught at his arm. His hands were icicle-cold.

"You gots to promise me one thing, Massa Austin," he said.

Austin nodded.

"You gots to promise me whatever you does, you gonna think it through real careful first. 'Cause that is what you do best, Massa Austin. No matter what you tryin' to prove, you thinks better'n anybody I ever seen. It's your gif'."

Austin kept his promise. After he'd crept down to Mousie's room to return the key and had crawled into his bed in his rose-wood and mahogany bedroom, he thought, and thought hard. When his head hurt from figuring and planning and reviewing, his mind wandered into a prayer.

Lord, I don't really expect You to help me for me. *I don't deserve it. But please, please help me for Henry-James. He feels called in Your Spirit. You can't turn Your back on that, can You?*

He didn't hear an answer. He'd already fallen asleep.

When he woke up the next morning, Charlotte had her nose almost touching his. Austin stiffened. If she was here to wrestle him down for what he did to Henry-James, he was pretty sure he'd lose.

"Wake up, sleepyhead," she said. "You're going to miss breakfast."

Even in his surprise, Austin looked up at the louvered shutters on his window. There was barely a thin trail of sunlight coming through.

"This early?" he asked.

"We're leaving at noon to go back to Canaan Grove," she said. "We have to eat now."

"No!" Austin cried.

He sat straight up in the bed and tore off the covers.

"I'm *ready* to go home," Charlotte said. "Daddy always acts so strange when we come here now. It's all this stupid war business."

"Strange?" Austin said. He turned his back to her and pulled a pair of pantaloons on over his sleeping drawers. "You think locking Henry-James in the attic is just 'strange'? I think it's—"

He stopped. There was no need to tell Charlotte that Henry-James was chained to the wall. She would never get over it. And he was surely not going to tell her that her beloved friend was planning to run away.

"It's what?" Charlotte said. She sat cross-legged on his bed. "You know Daddy has done things like this before and we thought something terrible was going to happen. But now I know he just gets upset about things and loses his temper. He'll never beat

Henry-James again after what happened last year, when Daddy accidentally hurt you, too."

"Are you mad at me for getting Henry-James in trouble this time?" Austin burst out. It wasn't a graceful way to change the subject, but it was all he could come up with.

Charlotte shook her head. "No, it's going to be all right. I know it. It'll all be fine as soon as we get home—away from all this hating." She fiddled with a strand of her hair. "Have you noticed it, Austin? Everywhere you look here, there's hate. I don't like Charleston anymore."

Austin sank down beside her and tried to act as if he were thinking that over. But his mind was grasping and plucking after one thought—how was he going to get to Kady before they all left for Canaan Grove?

"Anyway," Charlotte said, "I have a plan for this morning."

"What?" Austin said. His heart was starting to race. The first thing he had to do was get Charlotte occupied.

"I want you to help me get the key to the attic from Mousie so I can take some good food to Henry-James."

"No!"

Charlotte sat straight up. "I have to, Austin! Daddy has probably told Josephine to feed him some old mush-and-water thing."

"No, I mean, it's too dangerous for *you* to do it."

If Austin let Charlotte get into that attic and see Henry-James chained up like a dog, Henry-James never *would* forgive him for that.

"You're probably right," Charlotte said. "How can you be so smart about some things and so . . . well, anyway, how about this idea?"

Austin nodded vaguely as he went on thinking. Too bad Henry-James was chained up or he could lock Charlotte in the attic *with* him and then run off to Kady's and perhaps be back by noon.

"What if we set up a pulley system," Charlotte was saying. "Like you showed me when we had that problem at the well that time? There's an old cage in the shed—we could put food in there and run it up to him. Everyone's so busy getting ready to go back to Canaan Grove—and Daddy's brooding in his library—who would even know?"

Austin felt himself grinning. "Perfect," he said. "I'll go out and gather up all the things we need. You go get some food. Then come to the bushes in back."

Charlotte nodded happily and bounced off the bed. "And I know everything's going to be fine once we get away from here and get back to Canaan Grove," she said. "It's just this hateful place."

Austin just kept nodding as he ushered her out of the room. The minute she went on down the front stairs, Austin grabbed his jacket and hat and hurried down the back.

I can't lie to her—I have to do what I said I'd do, he thought. He ran to the gardening shed and found the cage Charlotte was talking about. It was big—they could send food for three weeks up in that. Although it didn't really matter. Unless Charlotte could figure this out herself, no food was going up—because Austin was going to be gone by the time Charlotte got to the bushes with muffins and preserves.

A quick search revealed some rope and a weight. Austin dragged it all to the bushes and left it there. Then, buttoning his jacket securely against the brisk March-morning chill, he hurried down the drive and out to the street.

I sure wish I could ride a horse, he thought as he crossed down to the wharves. *Or drive a buggy*.

He felt a sudden stormy wave. Why hadn't his father taught him things like that?

Maybe Ria was right. Maybe he wasn't a real man—if he wouldn't even come and get his family.

Austin shook that off. This walk was going to take forever. Especially since he had to go out of his way to keep from being noticed by anyone. The wharves were the perfect place for that. With people rushing back and forth with kegs on their shoulders or bags dragging behind them, no one had time to wonder what a 12-year-old boy was doing wandering around. At least it wasn't raining—and at least Concord Street was lonely this morning.

He went on trying to think of things that didn't bring on the storm inside him as he half walked, half ran north, toward the dark, shady, out-of-the-way part of town where Kady and Fitz lived.

"North of Broad Street—how utterly dreadful," Aunt Olivia would say if she knew. Aunt Olivia was convinced that anyone who didn't live south of Broad wasn't worth knowing.

By the time Austin reached the railroad tracks, he was ready to shed his wool jacket. Sweat was prickling against his skin, and he was puffing for air.

Uncle Drayton could make this hike without even getting out of breath, Austin thought. *So could Henry-James. So could Jefferson, for pity's sake!*

He made his way between the parallel sets of tracks. It was a wide-open space with no houses, and he tried not to look like a thief as he slipped from tree to tree. If he could just get past Moultrie Street, he was probably home free.

No sooner had he thought that than a sudden burst came from the bushes—a barking burst that came from a pack of drooling, snapping dogs.

✜ ✦ ✜

Chapter Ten

He was surrounded by them. There were so many that he couldn't tell where one set of fangs ended and another began. The starved-looking animals pranced and leaped and thrust themselves at him with hatred in their eyes.

Austin froze, moving only once to put his hands in front of his face. But his brain wasn't paralyzed. He could almost hear Virgil Rhett shouting, "We have special Negro-tracking dogs now that can pick up the scent of one of those wild desperadoes from just a scrap of fabric."

He couldn't have felt less like a wild desperado at that moment. One of the dogs caught at his sleeve with his long, pointy canine teeth and another scraped his paw all the way down the front of Austin's jacket. He stood like a piece of petrified wood and thought in terror, *Now I'm going to die. I didn't die on the pier—because I'm going to die now.*

"It looks as if we have one, captain!" someone shouted over the din.

Even in his frozen state, Austin thought there was something familiar about the voice. He knew he was right the minute a young man in a Confederate uniform emerged from a stand of trees, his very blond hair brushed forward beneath his kepi, his eyes sizzling blueness from under its brim.

It was Garrison McCloud, one of Kady's old suitors. The sight of him sent a thousand thoughts chasing each other through Austin's head.

He'll know me. He'll know I'm all right and he'll call his dogs off. But he knows I'm Uncle Drayton's Yankee nephew. He knows about my father. He probably knows he's a wanted man here.

He didn't know whether to give himself over to the dogs or stick out his hand and re-introduce himself to Garrison McCloud. He didn't have a chance to do either. Garrison stopped a few feet away, his eyes flickering with recognition. At once, he put his fingers to his mouth and gave a piercing whistle.

The dogs fell to whimpering. Some of them backed off immediately. Others seemed disappointed not to be given permission to take off one or two of Austin's fingers. They all eventually pranced away and charged back into the bushes as if they'd achieved some great victory.

"I know you, sir," Garrison said in his ever-so-proper southern voice.

Austin didn't answer. Better to find out if knowing him was a good thing or grounds for arrest.

"You're Drayton Ravenal's kin, am I right?"

"Yes, sir," Austin said. He drew up his shoulders. Something Kady had told him a while back curled through his head. *Act like you are where you're supposed to be, doing what you're supposed to be doing.*

Garrison flashed an instant smile and shook his head. "I thought surely we had a maroon. We don't usually get too many white people up this way unless they're up to no good. And being a Ravenal and all, I'm sure that doesn't apply to you."

"I'm not a Ravenal," Austin said. "I'm a Hutchinson."

He could have immediately bitten off his tongue as Garrison's smile disappeared and he crossed his meaty arms over his thick chest.

"Now that is so, isn't it?" he said.

"Yes," Austin said. He tried not to sound as panicked as he suddenly felt. *Why*, he thought, *did I have to go and remind him?*

"And that makes you an abolitionist, if I recall," Garrison said. He stepped a little closer, so that Austin could smell the rosewater on him. He kept himself from wrinkling his nose. No wonder Kady didn't want to marry him. He couldn't imagine Fitz sprinkling rosewater on himself.

"You wouldn't be about abolitionist business up here, now would you, Mr. Hutchinson?" Garrison said. He gave a cheerless laugh. "Of course, you wouldn't tell me anyway, now would you?"

"No,"Austin said, "I wouldn't."

"What do you have there?" someone else called from the trees.

"False alarm!" Garrison called back.

Austin's heart gave a leap. *He isn't going to arrest me. All right, that's a good sign.*

Garrison waited, as if to be sure the captain wasn't going to come out of the trees and see for himself. When all remained quiet except for the panting of the dogs, which they could hear even from there, the young soldier propped his foot up on a stump and directed his too-blue eyes at Austin. The way he puffed his chest out made his thick neck look even shorter. Austin wondered crazily if he would disappear inside his uniform jacket at any moment. He shook his head. He had to focus.

"I remember you very well now," Garrison said. "Kady's younger sister told me all about you. What was her name? Lucy?"

"Polly," Austin said.

"Poor thing," Garrison said. "I never saw a homelier girl—or one who tried so hard not to be."

Austin felt his shoulder blades start to prickle. "She's not so bad," he said.

"Well, I was never interested in her anyway. Kady was the one."

Austin hoped Garrison couldn't see him swallowing. He felt as if he were trying to get that squirrel-sized lump down his throat.

"All right, young fellow," Garrison said, his eyes suddenly taking on a new blaze. "I'm not sure what you're about up here, and I'm willing to wager it isn't something innocent. But I'm willing to let you go if you will tell me one thing."

"Think before you do anything, Massa Austin," he could hear Henry-James saying.

"I'm sure I could tell you a great many things you don't know," Austin said slowly. "Ask me anything you want."

"Is it true that Kady has gone and married a Yankee?"

Austin almost laughed in relief. As it was, his lips got trembly against his teeth.

"No," he said—honestly. "She hasn't married a Yankee. Did you hear that from the Fire Eaters?"

Garrison drew himself up. "It doesn't matter where I heard it."

"I'm just asking," Austin said, "because you might want to get more reliable sources. My cousin is *not* married to a Yankee."

"I knew it." Garrison was smiling again, and his chest was puffing out even farther, if that were possible. "I told them I sincerely doubted it, because as far as I could see, Miss Kady Ravenal wasn't going to marry at all."

"Oh, right," Austin said. "I mean, after all, she wouldn't marry *you*—and my Aunt Olivia certainly thought you were a catch."

Garrison nodded. Austin's shoulders relaxed. If he didn't have something so important to do, it might be fun to stay and tease poor unsuspecting Garrison McCloud some more.

But Austin cleared his throat and said, "Now, if you don't mind, I really would like to be getting on. We're returning to

Canaan Grove today, the family and I."

"Well now, you have a safe trip, do you hear? And please give Miss Kady my regards."

"I'll do that," Austin said. He backed casually away, nodding all the while.

"You might even want to tell her that my offer still stands. With the war inevitable, she's more likely to be thinking about a husband now."

"I'm sure of it," Austin said—truthfully. "And you can bet it isn't going to be a Yankee."

Garrison grinned and went jauntily back to the trees, still smiling. Austin turned on his heel and tore toward Moultrie Street, looking back over his shoulder only once to be sure that Garrison McCloud was still so wrapped up in himself that he hadn't realized Austin Hutchinson was going the wrong way.

He arrived at Kady's cabin puffing like a locomotive. He gave the secret knock, the one she'd taught him last winter, and waited only a moment before the door came open and Kady pulled him inside.

"Austin, what in heaven's name!" she said. "Did anyone see you come here?"

"No," Austin said. "They almost did, but I got away. Honest, no one suspects."

She nodded and put an arm around his shoulder. "I'm sorry. I'm just a little on edge these days, is all. There is so much happening." She cocked a dark eyebrow at him. "Which is, of course, why you're here, I would guess. What's wrong? Is it Daddy?"

As Austin poured out the story, Kady stoked the fire and poured him a cup of tea with milk and nodded every now and then. He was surprised that she didn't get up and start storming around the room or even throwing things.

When he was finished, she smoothed her hands out over her gray-and-white striped skirt.

"Daddy is near to losing his mind," she said. "He doesn't want this war—he's afraid he'll never see Aunt Sally or you boys again—and yet he's so afraid of losing his way of life, which he thinks is what makes him who he is." She shook her head. "You know more about who you are than he does about himself."

Austin snorted.

"What is that for?" she said. Her lips twitched.

"I know who I am, all right," he said. "I'm a bookish, unmanly little Wesley-boy."

"What?" Kady gasped, her teacup in mid-sip.

"There isn't anything wrong with that most of the time, I suppose," Austin said. "I can pretty much talk my way or think my way out of anything. But when it comes to being a real man, I guess that isn't what Jesus has in mind for me. I'm trying to accept that."

Kady put her cup into the saucer with a clatter. "And just how do you know at age 12 just exactly what Jesus has in mind for you, Austin Hutchinson?"

"Well, it's obvious, isn't it?"

"No, frankly, I think it's a surprise every day. You never cease to amaze me."

"You didn't see me yesterday, flapping from the pier like the Confederate flag." Austin stopped and squeezed his eyes shut tight for a second. "Let's not talk about this—let's talk about how we're going to set Henry-James free."

Now Kady got up and began to pace the room. When she hadn't spoken for a good five minutes, Austin's stomach started to churn.

"I thought you did this all the time," he said finally.

"I do," she said. "But not right out from under my father's nose. If Daddy is connected to me in any way, he could go to jail. And I've never done it for someone I care about as much as I do about Henry-James. He's like a brother to me—and to Charlotte."

"Does that mean you can't do it?"

"No. The word *can't* isn't in my vocabulary anymore, Austin. It just has to be done carefully. This may be our hardest one yet."

Austin looked around the cozy sitting room. "Where's Fitz?"

"Working," she said. "I'm going to have to consult him on this." She went on as if she were talking more to herself than to Austin. "We send most of our runaways to New York—they've had freedom for blacks there since 1827—but with so many already there, Henry-James won't have as many opportunities. If I could just get him to one of our free black conductors up there, though, we could send him on to Canada. . . ." She trailed off, then said, "Didn't you say you had to be back by noon?"

Austin sprang up out of the chair, slopping tea onto his pantaloons. "Yes! There are going to be a million questions!"

"And I'm sure you'll answer every one," Kady said, mouth twitching again. "All right, Austin, you have my wheels turning. I want you to go back to Henry-James and tell him that I am working on this—Fitz and I both are. He's not to worry about a thing. And he won't, once you tell him that you are going to be our contact person."

"What's a contact person?"

"We will get all information to you, and you will get it to Henry-James."

"But we're going back to Canaan Grove!"

"What's your point?" Kady said calmly. "Like you said—we do this all the time."

Austin grinned at her—and he was at once aware how good it felt to finally have something to smile about. He hadn't *really* smiled since before the pier.

He put his teacup on the table and reached for his jacket.

"Thank you," he said. "I'd better go now. I'll have to go the long way to avoid those dogs."

"What dogs?" Kady said. For the first time, she looked alarmed.

"Those 'Negro-tracking dogs' the soldiers have now for catching maroons."

"I know about those," Kady said. "I didn't know they went after white boys, too. I'd better drive you home in the wagon."

"You can't!" Austin said. "What if your father sees you? And what if some of the Fire Eaters see him with you?"

"And what if you get kidnapped again and there's no one to rescue you this time?"

Austin's heart sank a notch. "That's right," he said. "I'm not good at physical escapes."

"Oh, hush," she said. She twisted her mouth at him and reached for her bonnet and cape. "Just tell me where those dogs were."

He told her that—and also about Garrison McCloud as she drove the wagon away from the tracks toward Rutledge Avenue and then began to weave her way through town. At one point, she reached to the floor under her seat and pulled out a wide-brimmed man's hat.

"Put this on," she said. "Just to avoid any more trouble." She clicked her tongue. "And as if I'd marry that full-of-himself Citadel *brat*!"

As they drew closer to the townhouse on the East Battery, Austin grinned less and less and felt his stomach doing somersaults more and more. It wasn't Uncle Drayton's yelling or Aunt Olivia's chin-wiggling he was worried about. He had gotten used to that by now. It was Charlotte who was on his mind. If Kady said it once, she said it 20 times as they rode along: *Charlotte is to know nothing about this. She loves Henry-James so much that she won't be able to see anything else but how horrible it's going to be without him. Please, Austin.*

At least she wasn't sitting out in front of the house waiting for him. But there was a black buggy parked by the walkway, as if someone had driven up and rushed inside without bothering to tether his horse.

"Who would that be?" Austin said.

When Kady didn't answer, he looked at her. Her face was going white.

"That's the doctor's buggy," she said. "Someone's sick."

She didn't stop at the corner but pulled the wagon up behind the buggy and jumped down from the seat. Austin was hard put to keep up with her as she rushed in the front door.

Aunt Olivia was standing in the front hall, wringing out a lace handkerchief. Her face hardened like plaster when she saw Kady.

"What are *you* doing here?" she said.

"Oh, Mama, stop this," Kady said. "Who is ill? Why is the doctor here?"

Aunt Olivia sniffed. "As if you cared."

Kady gave an impatient sigh and brushed past her mother toward the stairs.

"He's not up there—he's in the library," Aunt Olivia said, "examining your father."

Kady whirled around on the third step, her face ashen. Austin could feel his heart starting to thunder.

"Daddy?" Kady said. "Why? Was he hurt?"

"Oh, yes," Aunt Olivia said. "Wounded to the very core of his soul—by you."

⚜

Chapter Eleven

"**I** don't understand," Kady said.

"Would it matter if you did?" Aunt Olivia said.

As far as Austin could see, she was enjoying herself, the way she was holding her chins so still.

"Mama, please, is Daddy all right?"

"If he is, it is no thanks to you," Aunt Olivia said. She put out her hand, and Mousie plunked a hanky into it. Aunt Olivia proceeded to dab at her very dry eyes. "The doctor says it's his heart—racing like a thoroughbred horse because of all the strain he's under."

"Kady's not the one who's trying to start a war!" Austin cried. "She's not spying on him like the Fire Eaters!"

Aunt Olivia's eyes flashed at him. Austin's heart took a dive.

"What do you mean by that?" she said. "Spying on Drayton—whatever for?"

"What I meant was—"

"What you meant was to stir up trouble, as usual. Having you and your mother and your little brother away from here isn't going to hurt his health any, that's for sure."

At least her attention to him had given Kady a chance to slip by and get to the library. Aunt Olivia swished off after her. Behind

97

him, on the stairs, someone sniffled. Austin looked up to see Polly with a handkerchief over her eyes and Tot standing by with a fresh one.

"He's dying, Austin," she said. "He's dying—I know it."

"I don't think so," he said.

"Yes, I can just feel it!"

With a loud sob, she stumbled down three steps and sagged against Austin. He stuck his arms out like a scarecrow and stared down at her head.

"I don't feel it," he said. All he could feel was his face going hot and red.

"Really?" she said. "Or are you just saying that so I won't become hysterical?"

That hadn't even occurred to him. He put his hands on her shoulders to stiffly push her away. She grabbed on to his wrists and searched his face with a pair of red-ringed eyes.

"Tell me the truth, Austin," she said. "I can take it."

"I don't know the truth," he said. "Except if it were really serious, your mother would be fainting dead away. Besides, I've read about hearts. Just because one is beating faster than normal doesn't mean it's diseased or anything. The doctor will probably prescribe bed rest and quiet."

Polly closed her eyes and rested her forehead against Austin's. He could feel his eyes bulging.

"You are such a comfort, Austin," she said.

I'm glad you're comforted, Polly, he thought. *I never felt more* un*comfortable in my life!*

He could have jumped for joy when the library door creaked open and Polly whipped past him in a whirl of taffeta to meet Kady coming out. Her face was grim. Behind her, Aunt Olivia's was near to purple.

"I think that settles it," Aunt Olivia was saying. "You heard the doctor."

"Heard what?" Polly said. "What did he say?"

"He said your father is not to have any upsets—anything that might put a strain on his heart. That means you are to stay away, Kady Sarah. Far away."

Austin opened his mouth to protest, but Aunt Olivia wasn't finished.

"Ever since you left, I have considered Polly my eldest daughter. I think this seals it. She has done nothing but please her father—and you have done nothing but tear him apart. If you want to do him any good now, you will forget you ever knew him."

Kady didn't even look at her. Face as stiff and white as a frosted pane, she gathered her cape around her and made for the front door. It slammed behind her, rattling the windows and shaking the bric-a-brac on the what-not.

Aunt Olivia gave a loud sniff and held out her hand to Polly. Austin suddenly couldn't stand to be there. He darted out the front door and ran to the wagon, where Kady was lifting the reins and clucking to the horse.

"She's a horrid witch!" Austin said.

"Never mind," she said in an icy voice. "We have work to do, Austin. Watch for my message."

And with a squeak of the wagon, she was gone.

Her words were the only thing that moved Austin back toward the house. But even then he wouldn't go in the front door for fear of seeing Aunt Olivia and saying something ugly. He wandered down the drive along the side of the house and let himself in the garden gate. Only then did he remember Charlotte.

She's probably crying somewhere, worried to death over her father, he thought. *If I can comfort Polly, I can sure comfort her.*

He broke into a run to the joggling board, but she wasn't there. Nor was she in any of their other usual places. He was about to go in through the French doors into the sitting room when he remembered her plan to get food to Henry-James.

I think I know how Uncle Drayton's heart must have felt, he thought as he moved toward the back of the house and his own heart began to thump at double-speed. It was a full-of-dread kind of heartbeat that left his stomach feeling queasy and his throat clogged.

Sure enough, she was there, sitting against the house with a large cage and a piece of rope and a bundle of what most certainly had been breakfast. She was staring straight ahead.

Austin stood there a minute. Then he cleared his throat. Then he said, "Hello."

She didn't move. Dragging his legs as if they were lead pipes, he got beside her and sat down.

"Your father's going to be all right," Austin said. "It's just heart strain—he just has to have peace and quiet—"

"Where did you go?" she said.

Austin was startled. Her voice didn't sound angry. It was flat and cold.

"I had to run an errand," he said. *His* voice hesitated like a child at a harpsichord.

"Where?"

"I can't tell you."

Then she turned on him. Her golden-brown eyes had a flash he'd never seen there before. For the first time, he saw her father in her.

"Why not, Austin?" she said. "I thought we were best friends. I thought we told each other everything. I thought you were the one person left I could depend on."

"I am!"

"Then why won't you tell me! Is it private?"

You can't lie to her, he thought. *That's something you just can't do.*

It was like his own voice calling to him. It was strong, and it felt right. Sadly, he shook his head.

"Not really, but it is a secret," he said.

"Why can't you tell me?"

"Because you can't know."

Charlotte got up and stood over Austin, trembling and rolling her skirt in her hands as if she were trying to strangle it. Austin gulped.

"Why?" she said. "Why can't I know?"

"Don't ask me that," Austin said. "Please—all right? At least I'm not lying to you. I could be making up some kind of story."

"I don't want some kind of story. I want the *real* story!"

"I can't tell you," Austin said.

He could barely get the words out, but for once shy Charlotte was having no trouble talking. She spat out her next sentence like a snake spewing venom.

"I told you, Austin," she said. "Everything here is hateful. Even you." She turned to run and stopped herself only long enough to add, *"Especially* you."

Austin tried to tell himself that she would calm down. That once she came to her senses, she would forgive him. That somehow she would understand. But after three days of silence, it became harder and harder to believe.

Those might have been the worst three days of his life so far. The doctor forbade Uncle Drayton to return to Canaan Grove, and although Drayton declared that no one "forbade" him to do anything, he stayed in bed in the Charleston townhouse, away from everyone.

Without him to rein in Aunt Olivia, she took full, vocal charge of the house. She seemed to be everywhere, yelping out orders and laying down rules. She made it difficult for Austin to get hold of the key to the attic at least once a day to feed Henry-James and keep his hopes up that Kady would come through.

The first day he had to use Jefferson's trick and bring in some Spanish moss, long enough to get a few fleas in the house. Once

Aunt Olivia got her first bite, she made Mousie give her a bath, which allowed Austin time to slip away with the key.

Another day, like Jefferson had, he yanked the bell pull and hid. When Mousie set down her basket to open the door, he scooped his hand in.

After the third day, he realized that no one else was going up to the attic besides Josephine, who was using Uncle Drayton's key, so he kept it under the featherbed in his room.

He practically starved himself at most meals so he could slip bread and fruit and other tidbits into his napkin and sneak them up to Henry-James. But Henry-James only picked at the food, and Austin usually ended up eating his share while they talked.

"When Miz Kady gonna send you a message?" he said on the third day.

"As soon as she can figure out the safest way to get you out," Austin said. "And she knows what she's doing, Henry-James, don't you worry."

"I ain't worried none—for me."

"Who *are* you worried for?"

"Miz Lottie. She can't know 'bout this, Massa Austin—now you promised me that."

"I did, and I'm keeping that promise," Austin said.

"I be thankin' you for that."

Austin stopped nibbling at a pickled cucumber and studied it. "You're welcome," he said. "You still feel called in spirit?"

"Uh-huh. I do."

"What does that feel like?"

Henry-James considered that for a minute. "It just a feelin', Massa Austin," he said. "You gets the thought in your head and then it jus' feel like . . . like you can't do nothin' else."

Austin set the cucumber down. "I just wanted to know because I'll never feel that."

"Why not?"

"Because I don't deserve it."

"Why wouldn't Marse Jesus give you that?" Henry-James said.

"Because I'm not satisfied with who He's made me to be."

"I don't know nothin' 'bout that," Henry-James said. His face twisted into a question mark.

"Of course you don't," Austin said. "Why would you want to be any different than you are? You're smart and strong and can do just about anything."

Henry-James looked solemnly at the chain around his neck and clinked it against the wall.

"Okay, so you can't right now," Austin said. "But you will soon. Kady is going to get a message to me any day now, I know it."

They sat in silence for a moment, until the attic became like a tomb. Austin was glad when the sound of clopping hoofbeats broke in from below. Austin went to the window, and he had to clap his hands over his mouth to keep from calling out.

"That Miz Kady?" Henry-James said.

Austin felt a pang for him. "No, it's my mother . . . and Jefferson . . . Bogie . . . and your mother!"

"No," Henry-James said.

"Well, yes, it is. I know Ria when I see her."

"No, Massa Austin, she can't know 'bout me bein' chained up here."

"Come on, Henry-James! What am I supposed to tell her when she asks where you are?"

"You can tell her I's in the attic, but nothin' 'bout no chain, you hear?"

"You have my word," Austin said.

But the promise settled on him like a weight. Charlotte was one thing, but Ria was quite another. When those eyes drove into a person—

Austin hurried out of the attic and downstairs before he could be missed. His mother pulled him into her arms and half sighed, half laughed—and cried a little—into his hair.

"And to think I was going to send you off without me at one time," she said to him. "I couldn't bear it—not for a single day."

Austin wriggled out of her hug—women were certainly doing that a lot to him lately—and tugged her toward the stairs.

"I have so much to tell you," he said.

"Oh, not half as much as I have for you," she said. "Let me peek in on Drayton first and then we'll talk. Meet me in my room."

She handed him her wrap and went on up the stairs. Austin was left with Ria.

"You mind carryin' this here bag, Massa Austin?" she said.

Austin didn't look at her as he took the bag and went ahead of her up the stairs. He might as well have blurted everything out, though, for when they got to the room, she set down the bags, put her hands on her hips, and asked, "Where is Henry-James, Massa Austin?"

Austin concentrated on keeping his back to her. "He's in the attic," he said.

"Why?"

"Because Uncle Drayton wouldn't listen to me when I told him that Henry-James was only trying to *save* Charlotte and me—he wasn't the one who got us into trouble in the first place."

"Marse Drayton beat him?" she said.

"Oh, no, he's just keeping him locked up for a while."

"How long?"

"I don't know."

"But you knows something, Massa Austin," she said. "You sure 'nuff do."

With that she busied herself with putting Mother's clothes away. Austin slipped out while he could.

He wasn't able to talk to his mother until later that afternoon, and by then she was as disturbed as he had ever seen her. Ria was in Uncle Drayton's room, where she had been reassigned, and Jefferson was in the garden petting Bogie, who was tethered to a long chain.

"That child has been a monster," Mother said. "Uncle Drayton feels the strain in his heart, and Jefferson feels it in that part of him that makes him impossible! The only way we could get him onto that boat was if we brought Bogie along. Olivia may *never* speak to me again—which might not be all that bad, actually."

"Maybe Jefferson will be better here," Austin said.

"I wouldn't hold my breath. He's even worse here than at Canaan Grove."

"Is Uncle Drayton sicker than the doctor told us?" Austin said.

"No, I think he'll be up and around soon. It's his mind I'm concerned about. He's so confused. I have never known my brother to be unsure about what to believe, what to do. I know that's why he shut Henry-James away. The boy is a constant reminder that this war, this slavery issue, none of this is right."

"Did you try to talk him into letting Henry-James out?"

"Of course. And I got nowhere. That's what worries me. I've always been able to get through to Drayton before." She sighed. "I'll keep hammering away at him, but we don't have much time."

Austin's heart seemed to stop beating altogether.

"Why not?" he said.

"I've heard from your father," she said.

Austin couldn't remain sitting. He jumped off the bed and paced the floor—just like Kady.

"Austin, be calm," Sally Hutchinson said. "We aren't leaving today. I don't know when we're going, exactly. Your father only said for me to come to Charleston—which was fine because Uncle Drayton needs Ria here. Father said there will be ships coming to bring supplies to Fort Sumter. We will receive word exactly when, and we are to be at Charleston harbor to await an escort."

"How much time do you think I have?" Austin said.

Mother reached out to him as he passed the bed and made him sit down. She took both his fists in her hands.

"Austin, what is it?" she said. "I know you don't want to leave everyone, but we've been down this road before. This is something more than hating to say good-bye, isn't it?"

Austin opened his mouth to deny it, but then the thought sprang into his mind, *Don't lie. She's your friend.*

"Did you ever feel like there was something you had to do, even if it didn't make sense?" he said.

She tapped Austin's fists against each other as she thought. "I have, especially since we've been here. I've felt I had to help Kady—and certainly I needed to try to dissuade your uncle from his path." She smiled at him. "And I felt called to be a mother when I learned you were going to be born. You are the best choice I've ever made, Austin—you and your brother."

Austin tried not to roll his eyes. Why did everyone insist on turning everything into a crying party right now? There was work to be done!

"So what do you feel called to do, Austin?" she said.

He didn't even hesitate this time. "I have to help Henry-James—and I can't tell either Charlotte or Ria about it."

Both of Mother's eyebrows went up. That made Austin's stomach churn again.

"You don't think I can do it?"

"My love, that isn't the question. It won't be *you* who's doing it." She squeezed his hands and then let them go.

Austin felt a little more peaceful after that. He left his mother to rest and went into the upstairs sitting room, where he could look out over the sunny street. March was almost over, and the Battery was lined with trees flowering in fluffy array.

He'd no more than settled himself in to sort things through, however, when footsteps sounded behind him. He didn't even have to turn around to know it was Charlotte.

"Austin!" she said.

"Lottie!" he cried. "I knew you'd come around—"

"Hush *up*, Austin, and listen to me! I think Tot is about to do something *terrible*!"

✢ ✢ ✢

Chapter Twelve

"Don't tell me she's starting another fire in the kitchen!" Austin said.

Charlotte could only shake her head.

"Then what?" Austin said. "Charlotte, you're scaring me."

"*I'm* scared! I went in the kitchen to get a sugar candy lump and Tot was in there by herself."

"Why wasn't she with Polly?"

"I don't know, but Austin, she was grinding mushrooms into a powder."

"Mushrooms?"

"Those ones she picked at Canaan Grove."

Austin got up slowly from his chair. "What did she do with it?"

"I didn't stay to see—I came to get you. She had the most awful look on her face, Austin!"

"Come on," Austin said.

Together they raced down the back steps, out the back door, and down the path to the kitchen building. Austin stopped Charlotte by the window.

"Maybe we should watch from here," he said. "You know how she gets hysterical when we startle her."

Charlotte nodded. They ducked below the windowsill and slowly stood up enough to peer in. Austin stifled a gasp.

"Does your mother usually have mushrooms in her tea?" he whispered.

"Of course not!"

"Then I think you're right, Lottie—she *is* doing something terrible!"

Austin was up even before Charlotte, who sprang to action like a rabbit. Austin flung open the door and ran into the kitchen with Charlotte on his heels. Tot drew back her hand, now poised over Aunt Olivia's teacup, and began to stutter. Her eyes looked ready to pop right out of her head.

"I wasn't doin' nothin', Miz Lottie!" she said in her fingernail-scraping voice. "I's just fixin' Miz Livvy's tea!"

"You never fix Mama's tea," Charlotte said. "That's Mousie's job."

"I's just fixin' Miz Livvy's tea!" she said again.

Austin gave an exasperated sigh. "We know that part, but what did you put in it? Mushrooms, wasn't it?"

Tot let out a shriek that topped her highest one yet and dropped to the floor with a thud so hard that it clattered the pans hanging on hooks on the wall.

"She slap Miz Polly!" she cried. "She done haul off and slap Miz Polly! Evil! E-*vil*!"

Charlotte hurried to one side of her, Austin to the other. After two tries, they were able to haul her to her feet and get her to the bench by the fireplace. Tot was sobbing in hiccups that wrenched her *and* them.

"Mama slapped Polly?" Charlotte said when she could be heard over Tot's wailing.

Tot nodded—about 20 times.

"For what?" Charlotte said.

"For nothin'!" Tot cried. She was beginning to wind up again. "For nothin' a'tall!"

"I believe that," Austin said. "Aunt Olivia's been worse than ever since Uncle Drayton took sick."

"But Tot," Charlotte said, pointing to the teacup, "that's no reason to *poison* her!"

Tot began to shake her head, and Austin was sure she was going to do nothing *but* shake it until she keeled over. But she managed to squeeze a few more words out.

"I jus' want her to be good an' sick," she said. "Lord, help me—I jus' want her to be sick so she leave Miz Polly alone."

"No, Tot," Charlotte said. "That's only going to get you in trouble. Do you want to end up in the attic like Henry-James?"

Tot started the head-shaking again. Austin grabbed her chin.

"All right, Tot," he said firmly. "We're going to dump out that tea, and we're going to make some more."

"*We?*" Charlotte said.

"All right, *Charlotte* is going to make some more—and we're never going to say anything about this to anybody, right?"

Tot sniffed loudly and nodded.

"But you have to promise never—ever—to try anything like this again," Charlotte said. "You don't want Daddy to sell you or something, do you?"

That seemed to have the biggest effect yet. Tot bolted up from the bench with her lips flapping.

"No, Miz Lottie!" she cried. "I can't live without my Polly! No, Miz Lottie!"

"Then no more mushrooms in people's tea," Austin said.

The kitchen door opened, and Austin knew all three of them must have looked as if they'd just tried to do away with the entire household. Fortunately, it was Mousie, who was too busy clasping and unclasping her hands to notice.

"Miz Livvy want her tea," she said.

"Coming right up!" Austin said gaily. "Go tell her something special is being prepared."

Mousie nodded nervously and squeaked her way out the door.

Charlotte was staring at him. "Something special?" she said.

"We'll think of something," Austin said. "We always do."

The one good thing that came out of Tot's attempt on Aunt Olivia's health was that Charlotte was talking to him again. It was a brittle, cautious kind of talking, but Austin didn't jiggle it.

He certainly didn't bring up the subject of Henry-James or what Tot's plan had made him think about.

Tot should run away, too, he thought over and over when he was reviewing the day and talking to Jesus at night. *It's only a matter of time before Uncle Drayton and Aunt Olivia sell her.*

But what would that do to her—and to Polly? They were as attached to each other as Henry-James and Charlotte.

I hope this is right, Lord, Austin prayed. *Because it's sure going to break a lot of hearts.*

But Jesus didn't appear to be anxious to let him know. Austin seemed to be waiting endlessly—for Kady to send a message, for Father to send word to them, for Jefferson to stop driving everyone to distraction, for Aunt Olivia to stop tempting her own fate by nagging at Polly.

"Why doesn't something happen?" he asked Henry-James one evening.

"I been wondering that myself, Massa Austin," he said. "I surely have, and I think we just got to keep on prayin'. You bring any more water?"

Austin nodded and handed Henry-James the bottle. He leaned his head back and drained it.

"You sure are drinking a lot," Austin said. "You want me to get you some more?"

Henry-James shook his head. "Somebody might could suspect somethin' if'n you do. My mama, she been askin' 'bout me?"

"Yes, but Aunt Olivia won't even let her near here. She says Ria has to be by Uncle Drayton's side every minute, even though he's sitting up writing letters and reading books and everything."

"That's all right with me," Henry-James said. "Jus' so my mama don't see these here chains."

He ran his hand across his mouth and gave a shiver. "You think next time you could bring me a blanket, Massa Austin—without nobody seein' you?"

"I think there must be one up here," Austin said.

He uncovered several from the trunks that were nearby and wrapped them around Henry-James—although he wasn't sure why. His slave friend was glowing with sweat, as if he'd been working in the rice fields on a summer afternoon.

"I'll bring extra water next time," Austin said.

Is he sick? Austin wondered as he sneaked once more out of the attic and down to his room.

But the thought scampered off when he climbed into bed next to a sleeping Jefferson and heard something smack against his window.

At first he wasn't sure it was anything more than a bird. But when it came again, he crept out of bed and pulled aside the drape to look down into the garden. There didn't appear to be anyone there, but one of the boxwood bushes began to shiver in a frenzy. Austin paused. There was no breeze that night.

Trying hard not to make a sound, Austin pushed open the window and leaned as far out as he dared. Something white came up out of the boxwood and rested on its top. A piece of paper? Cloth?

Whatever it was, it was obvious he was supposed to go down and investigate.

It was chilly outside, and Austin hadn't bothered to put anything on over his light drawers and sleeping shirt. Holding his bare feet stiff against the damp ground, he crept to the boxwood and picked up the small scrolled piece of paper. Whoever had put it there was now gone.

Although Austin shivered, he quickly forgot how cold he was when he unrolled the paper.

We can take delivery on that package you have for us. Would be helpful if you could have it unwrapped.

Austin turned the paper over, but there was nothing more on the back.

It has to be from Kady and Fitz, he thought. *They're coming for Henry-James, and they want me to unchain him. But how?*

For a minute, he groped around in his mind for an idea. Everyone was telling him that thinking was what he did best. He had to think now.

But nothing seemed to come.

He couldn't tell Henry-James that, however. As he hurried back to the attic and unlocked the door, he told himself over and over, *I can't let him give up hope.*

"You bring more water?" Henry-James whispered to him.

"No, I bring good news," Austin said. "I heard from Kady. It's going to happen soon."

He stopped there, but Henry-James seemed to read his mind.

"How they gonna get me out with this here chain on me?" he asked.

"I'm . . . I'm thinking about that," Austin said.

Henry-James pulled the blankets tighter around him and watched Austin's face.

"Are you feeling better?" Austin said.

"I ain't sick, Massa," Henry-James said. "I's jus' all fitful 'cause I gots to be up here."

"That's a relief, at least," Austin said. "I thought you had the malaria or something. . . ."

His lips kept moving, but no more sound came out. His mind was shooting off in another direction.

"You all right, Massa Austin?" Henry-James asked.

"I'm very all right," Austin said. He scrambled to his feet. "Do you want to play one last pretend game with me, Henry-James?"

"This ain't no game, Massa—" Henry-James started to say.

But even in the dark, Austin saw a gleam come into his eyes. "What game you got in mind, Massa Austin?"

Austin could feel his own eyes gleaming. "Here's what we'll do," he said.

At first, Henry-James refused. Austin had to do his toughest talking yet. Finally, Henry-James gave in—as long as his mother wasn't let in on the secret.

It was dark and quiet in the rest of the house as Austin came down from the attic for the second time that night. He tiptoed to Uncle Drayton's room and listened outside the door. Silence.

Slowly, he pushed open the door just a crack before Ria jumped up from the chair where she'd been nodding. In the background, Uncle Drayton was snoring evenly.

"Massa Austin, you 'bout scared me half to death," she whispered.

"Sorry," Austin whispered back. "But I think you'd better come to the attic. Henry-James is bad-off sick."

Ria gasped—something Austin had seldom heard. It was loud enough to set Uncle Drayton stirring in his bed.

"You got a key?" she whispered.

Austin waited until they were just outside the attic door to prepare Ria.

"You need to know this," he said. "Henry-James is chained."

He couldn't see Ria's face, but he could feel her stillness in the dark. It was as eerie as the calm he'd sensed that day before the big storm at the pier.

"I's ready for it, Massa Austin," she said finally. "I's ready to see my boy."

Austin was still a little uneasy, but he needn't have worried.

The performance Henry-James gave went beyond what he'd hoped for. He was curled up in a ball, sweating heavily under his blankets and gasping for air.

"Do you think it's malaria?" Austin whispered to Ria.

She knelt to touch him, but Henry-James shook himself away.

"I gots to go see Marse Drayton" was all she said.

She hurried toward the door, and Austin followed, risking one glance over his shoulder at Henry-James. The black boy stopped shivering long enough to give Austin a nod. So far, so good.

Uncle Drayton was none too happy to be awakened—and he was even less delighted when he found out Ria had been in the attic.

"I was told he was ill, Marse," Ria said. "I thought since I's the nurse, I ought to—"

"So how sick is he?" Uncle Drayton asked.

"Bad," Ria said. "Fever's got him near out of his mind. He don't even know me."

Uncle Drayton scowled. "Ria, this had better not be some ploy of yours to get your boy out of the attic, because—"

"She can care for him in the attic," Austin said quickly.

Uncle Drayton started to frown at him, but Austin pushed on. "Don't you think, though, that he ought to be taken off his chain so he can lie down and get better?"

There. It was out. Now if only it would work.

Ria waited with that strange stillness. Austin tried to copy it and failed miserably. He couldn't keep himself from twitching. Uncle Drayton just sat and scowled.

"Well," he said at last, "I suppose he's worth nothing to me dead. The key is in the box on the bureau. Fetch it, Austin, and see that you bring it back."

Letting Henry-James out of his chain lifted Austin's hopes like nothing had for days. He left Ria with him—wiping his brow and talking soothingly to him. Austin couldn't help but laugh to himself.

Keep it up, Henry-James. Maybe you can be an actor in your new home.

When he was back in bed, he prayed again. *I've unwrapped the package, Lord. Now all I have to do is wait for another message from Kady.*

But the message that arrived at the Ravenal townhouse the next day wasn't from Kady or Fitz. It was from Wesley Hutchinson.

Be at the Charleston Harbor on April 10, it said.

April 10? Austin thought. *That's tomorrow.*

✛ ◆ ✛

Chapter Thirteen

One day. That was all he had. It was the closest Austin had ever come to losing hope.

"Why does it have to be so soon?" he asked his mother.

She turned from the bag she was folding Jefferson's clothes into and sighed.

"That's when the ships President Lincoln has sent are scheduled to arrive at Fort Sumter. The moment they've transferred the supplies to the fort, they'll be on their way back north again."

Austin raked his hand through his hair.

"You haven't been able to do what you want yet, have you?" she said.

"I need more than one day."

She snapped the bag shut and came to stand by Austin. Smoothing his hair down, she studied his face.

"Is there anything I can do to help?" she asked.

He couldn't see what. Now that Ria was with Henry-James all the time, Austin couldn't get to him. He wasn't at all sure how he was going to get her out of the way for Fitz to take Henry-James away, even if Austin could get word to Kady in time. The only good thing that had happened was that the minute they'd

117

gotten word from Father, Charlotte had run off to cry by herself. At least he didn't have to answer a lot of questions.

"You know I'll help however I can," Mother said.

Even if Austin had been able to think of something, it would have been wiped out by Jefferson's sudden entrance into the room.

"We're leaving?" he said.

"Yes, love. Tomorrow."

"Well, good-bye," he said. He gave his dark head a snap.

"What do you mean, good-bye?" Austin said. "You're going with us, shrimp."

"Not me!" Jefferson said. "I'm going to be Uncle Drayton's son and stay here."

"What?" Austin and his mother said in perfect unison.

"Just what I said. I don't want to go live with that weakling. I'm Uncle Drayton's little man."

"What weakling?" Mother said.

Austin had a sudden queasy feeling in his stomach.

"Father," Jefferson said matter-of-factly, as if he were answering the question, "What time is it?"

"Where on earth did you get such an idea?" Mother said. She looked as if someone had just slapped her in the face.

"Hush up, shrimp," Austin said. "Can't you see you're upsetting Mother?"

"No, I want to know about this," she said. "Come here, Jefferson."

More than anything, Austin wanted to bolt out of there and find his uncle. Why couldn't he be more careful what he said in front of Jefferson? He was too little to hear things like that.

"I heard it from Austin," Jefferson said.

Austin's heart screeched to a halt. Slowly, Sally Hutchinson pulled her eyes from Jefferson and let them move to Austin. The look in them made him want to crawl under the bed.

"I never said anything like that!" Austin said. That was true. He'd never spoken about his father that way to anyone.

"You did so," Jefferson said. "When you were praying. I heard you whispering it right out loud to God."

His mother was still staring at him. Austin could feel the skin on his cheeks burning.

"You must have been dreaming," he said.

"Was not either. You said, 'Jesus, I'll be a puffball weakling like my father, if You'll only help me with this one thing I have to do before I go'."

Austin looked helplessly at his mother. "I didn't—"

"Jefferson," she said, "you *will* be going with us to return to your father, and you can thank our good Lord that he *is* your father. He is a strong, brave, wonderful man. I hope you grow up to be just like him."

"I want to be like Uncle Drayton!"

"We'll talk about this later," she said. "Go on now and make sure you have a few toys to take with you."

"I'm telling Uncle Drayton. I'm telling him I don't want to go!"

Before she could grab him, Jefferson took off, flinging the door open and thundering off down the hall screaming, "Uncle Drayton!" in a voice that would have made even Tot cringe.

Austin was doing more than cringing. Every inch of his skin was on fire.

Mother went to the door and closed it. She didn't turn around to look at him as she spoke.

"Is that what you think of your father, Austin?" she asked.

"I never said that to anybody. He was eavesdropping on my prayers."

"But is that what you *think*, Austin?"

Austin licked his lips, which had gone painfully dry. "That isn't what I really meant. He just isn't a manly kind of person.

He reads books and gives lectures, and I admire him for that—I truly do. And I guess I'm like that, too, only I hoped I could be more than that. But it doesn't matter now—I'll be anything as long as I can help Henry-James."

"You can work all your life, Austin Hutchinson," she said, "and you will never be more than your father—because there *is* nothing more."

She finally turned to him, and his heart sank to his toes. She was crying.

"He's the finest man I know," she said.

"I know!" Austin said. "Even Uncle Drayton told me when we were leaving last time that Father was—"

"I really don't care one tiny bit what your Uncle Drayton thinks about Wesley Hutchinson," she said. She put her hands to the sides of her face and shook her head. "Austin, I thought you of all people recognized what the word *man* means. Have your father and I failed you completely?"

"No!"

She put her hand lightly over her mouth. "I think you'd better go, Austin. Go get your things packed. I can't talk about this right now."

Austin couldn't move.

"I'm sorry," he said. "I just—"

"Go, please. I think that's best just now."

Austin, the thinker, made a hasty retreat to the upstairs sitting room and curled himself into a ball on his favorite chair. But he hated all the thoughts that tumbled over each other in his head. Whoever Austin Hutchinson was or was meant to be, he hated it all.

I'm sorry, Lord, he kept thinking over and over. *I'm not who I want to be. I'm not who You want me to be. I can't finish what I need to do before I leave.*

And then a thought echoed back: *But the least you can do is try*.

It wound its way past all the thunderous noise and whispered something that made sense.

The least you can do is try.

Try what? Try to undo the hurt he'd done to his mother and Jefferson? Try to get word to Kady? At least let her know he was leaving tomorrow? Maybe there was something she could do before then.

Think, Austin, he scolded himself. *That's what you do so well*.

It seemed now that even his ability to think wasn't much of a "gif'." But it was all he had. He uncurled himself from the chair and went to the window. All right. Get to Kady's.

He thought hard. He saw Charlotte below, listlessly plucking blossoms off the peach tree and letting them blow away. She needed something to do to take her mind off things, too—and the farther away she was, the less Austin would hurt. The fewer hurts, the better.

He got to her before she left the yard.

"Lottie," he whispered breathlessly when he reached her, "I think you better go get Kady."

"Why?" she said.

"Because . . . it's worse with Henry-James."

Charlotte's eyes grew round. "Is he going to die?"

"Oh, no! But I think seeing Kady will help him."

Her face went so pale that Austin almost changed his mind. She grabbed his hand.

"Come with me!" she said. "We'll take one of the horses!"

"That's not a good idea, Lottie," he said quickly. "You know how I am on the back of a horse. I'm likely to slow us down."

She nodded—without hesitation.

That's all right, Austin thought glumly. *It's the truth. I'm the one who's the weakling*.

With Charlotte gone, Austin hurried back to the kitchen building. His hopes were rewarded—Ria was in there, fixing Henry-James's dinner. There should be time to get up to the attic and talk to him alone.

It was good to see his slave friend unbound and sitting by the window when he got there.

"Where Miz Lottie taking off to in such a hurry?" he said to Austin when he arrived.

"To get Kady," Austin said. "Listen, Henry-James, I have a new plan. Do you trust me?"

Henry-James didn't even stop to think. He nodded.

Even when Austin laid out his scheme, Henry-James was still nodding. There was pain in his eyes, though.

"Lot of people gonna be mad at you this way, Massa Austin," he said.

Austin shrugged miserably. "It doesn't matter," he said. "Right now, I think even Jesus is mad at me."

"Don't you think that," Henry-James said. "You Jesus' own boy, I knows it. You jus' keep on prayin'."

Austin stopped for a precious second to look at Henry-James. His eyes had a sad kind of wisdom in them.

"You know something, Henry-James?" he said.

"What's that?"

"You're starting to sound just like Daddy Elias. I don't care what he said before he died—I think he'd be proud of what you're doing."

"I hope so, Massa Austin," Henry-James said. "I sure hope so."

There were footsteps below. Austin crept out and into his hiding place in the dormer. Ria passed him without so much as a glance, and then Austin was down to the second floor and tapping on Uncle Drayton's door. There was an abrupt, "Come in."

Austin took a deep breath and forced himself to let it out hard. He burst through the door and hoped his face was red.

"Uncle Drayton!" he cried. "I have something to tell you!"

"Could you tell me in a lower voice?" Uncle Drayton said. "You'll have your aunt in here—"

He stopped himself, and Austin took the opportunity to jump right in.

"I was just up in the attic—"

"My order was that you were to stay away from there!"

"I know, but you should be glad I didn't follow that order, sir. Henry-James is only *pretending* to be sick!"

Uncle Drayton tightened the sash on his silk robe and narrowed his eyes at Austin. "What makes you think that?"

"Because he was strolling around the attic, pretty as you please. There isn't a thing wrong with him, Uncle Drayton. He only wants to make us all think he's sick, even Ria, so you won't sell him at the auction tomorrow."

"Tomorrow?"

"Since you're feeling so much better, I just assumed you'd go tomorrow if he wasn't so sick—which he's not."

Shadows fell, dark and menacing, across Uncle Drayton's face. Austin held his breath.

"I don't understand this," his uncle said finally. "I thought you fancied yourself a brother to Henry-James. Why would you bring me news like this?"

This was the hard part. But Austin was prepared for it. It was the only way he could think of, without having to lie.

"I think a person should do what's right, no matter how hard it is," he said.

It was as if Uncle Drayton had a ball in his head that he was tossing back and forth: Believe him. Don't believe him. Austin tried not to beg him with his eyes.

Then briskly he untied his sash and threw off the silk robe.

"I've been in this sickroom long enough," he said. "The entire place is going to seed on me." He went to his cupboard and pulled out a stiff white shirt with the collars only partially buttoned on. "Thank you, Austin," he said. "I'm sure this was difficult for you."

You don't know the half of it, sir, Austin thought.

He stood by the door and watched Drayton pull on his clothes. As soon as his uncle had stomped past him into the hall, Austin crept to the little box on the bureau and slid his hand inside. With the key tucked into his palm, he hurried out.

The next thing to do was get to the corner and wait for Kady and Charlotte. The horse arrived first with Charlotte on it, hair flying out behind her.

"How is he?" she shouted to Austin.

He sucked in a big breath of air. If he were going to let her in on his plan, now would be the time. But she would never agree. This had to be better. Hard as it was, this had to be better.

"You should go on in," he said.

Wild-eyed, she dug her heels into the horse's sides and galloped on to the house.

Kady drove her wagon furiously around the bend a few minutes later. Austin flagged her down and jumped up beside her.

"What's wrong with Henry-James?" she said. "Is he too sick to be transported?"

Austin shook his head and explained—trying to include only the most important details. She followed with her eyes, nodding and, he could tell, replanning.

"Good work, Austin," she said. She gave him a grim smile. "This is going to create some hate and discontent for you. But you'll make up with Charlotte once she understands."

"I don't think there's going to be time," he said. "We're leaving tomorrow."

"Ah," she said. "So that's why you've taken matters into your own hands." She gave his hand a single squeeze. "I'll miss you, Austin. I truly will." Then she pulled her hand away and sat up like a tidy little businesswoman. "All right, I will be in the alley behind Chalmers Street tomorrow at noon. Do you have that key?"

Austin uncurled his fingers and let the key slide into her hand. "I've never stolen anything before," he said.

"I told you once, Austin," she said. "If it takes robbing the slave masters to abolish slavery, I am proud to be called a thief."

Austin nodded. It was time to get out of the wagon, but he couldn't make himself do it.

"There was a reason why you couldn't leave Charleston that night last winter," Kady said to him. "I could feel it when we were out in that boat. Now, though, it feels right somehow. I think you've done all you can do here."

Austin shook his head. That lump the size of a squirrel was rising in his throat again. "I don't think so," he said. "But at least I tried."

She nodded. "That's all a man can do—try and pray."

As she drove off up the Battery again, Austin felt his feet turn to leaden blobs on the sidewalk. Returning to the house was going to be the hardest thing he'd ever had to do. Mother was already disappointed in him. Jefferson was making that worse. Ria and Charlotte were going to be ready to murder him.

I better check all my food for mushrooms, he thought.

But he couldn't make himself laugh.

And he was right. He didn't even get up to his room before Ria had him cornered. Her eyes were smoldering like two pieces of coal.

"I jus' 'bout let myself trust you like I done your Mama," she said. "Jus' show how wrong a person can be."

Austin didn't say a word.

When Mousie rang the bell for dinner, he dragged himself reluctantly to the table. He didn't care if Josephine had fixed pan dowdy *and* sweet potato pie, he couldn't imagine himself eating, not with Charlotte there asking questions with her eyes—or worse, not looking at him at all.

But it was worse than that. She wasn't even there. Polly was, and she had plenty to say.

"I don't understand you, Austin Hutchinson," she hissed to him in the doorway. "My sweet sister is up in her room sobbing her heart out. I would be surprised if she lasted through the night, broken as her heart is."

I thought you were a Confederate girl through and through, he wanted to say to her. But it didn't matter. Nothing seemed to matter now. The only thing that was going to make him ever like himself again was to get Henry-James to freedom.

He turned away from the dining room and went back upstairs.

Darkness couldn't come soon enough, and the minute it did, Austin started to climb into bed. He was met with two cold feet in his back.

"Move over, shrimp," he said.

"Don't call me shrimp," Jefferson said. "Don't call me anything."

"All right. Just get your feet out of the way so I can go to sleep."

"No. I don't want you in here with me. You squealed on Henry-James. You aren't my brother anymore."

"I was acting like Uncle Drayton!" Austin snapped at him. "I thought you worshipped Uncle Drayton."

"I don't care," Jefferson said. He thrust out his lower lip and stared Austin down—and he didn't move his feet.

With a sigh, Austin snatched up a bolster and a blanket and went out into the hall. He'd barely gotten settled on the floor when his mother's door across the hall opened, and he heard her gasp.

"Austin, what on earth?"

"Jefferson hates me," he said. "I don't even blame him."

"Come in here at once. Honestly!"

"Is Ria in there?" Austin said.

Mother shook her head. "I told her to go sleep in the slaves' quarters where she can be alone."

Austin nodded and followed her into her room. He headed straight for a chair and curled up in it with his back to her.

"What's this now?" she said.

"So you don't have to look at me," he said.

"And why wouldn't I want to look at you?"

"Because I'm hateful."

"Are you talking about Henry-James?"

"That's part of it."

She came to sit where she could face him, and she tilted his chin up out of the blanket with her fingers. Her face twitched into a smile.

"You're up to something with that. I didn't tell Ria, though I wanted to. Is this how you're helping him?"

Austin nodded.

"Aren't you mad at me, though? Don't you hate me because of what I said about Father?"

"Hate you? Austin, where do you get these ideas? I was hurt . . . disappointed. But I've been thinking about it this afternoon, and I know the reason for you thinking the way you do about your father. You don't even know him." She smiled at him. "But I think we have enough going on right now, my love. It'll take a long time for you to get over leaving Charlotte and the rest of them, I know that. It's a shame you have to leave them with all this resentment and anger going on, but I know you have a reason. I'm just so sorry, my love."

He could feel his face crumpling, and that was the last thing he wanted her to see. She nodded as if she knew that and pulled him to her, where he could sob without a sound and they could both pretend it wasn't happening. He fell asleep with his head still in her lap.

He woke up before it was light, to the sound of rain whipping against the window in sheets. Mother was already up, wrapping her robe around her and hurrying to open the shutters to look out.

"Oh, my!" she said.

Austin stumbled over to look. The street was already rushing like a river, and when the lightning flashed, he could see that the palm trees on the Battery were nearly bent in two.

There was a knock on the door, and Polly flew in, eyes wild, with Tot, of course, clinging to her nightgown.

"The whole household is already up," Polly said. "Daddy says this is the worst storm he's ever seen in Charleston."

"I believe it," Mother said. She put her arm around Polly.

"And I'm glad," said another voice from the doorway.

Austin jumped. It was Charlotte—hair tousled but chin up.

"What a wretched thing to say!" Polly said.

"No, it isn't," Charlotte said. She looked right at Austin. "This means Daddy won't be able to go to the auction today. He's already said."

She turned on her bare heel and walked out—leaving Austin with his heart trying to tear its way out of his chest.

✛ ⊶✛⊷ ✛

o auction. No Kady. No more chances to help Henry-James get free.

The storm outside was nothing compared to the thoughts churned up inside Austin. He grabbed the front of his nightshirt, just to be sure his chest didn't explode.

"Well, Austin," Mother said. "I think you may have had your prayers answered." She looked at him with clouds in her own eyes. "I don't think many ships will be getting to Fort Sumter in this storm."

For the third time, the door flew open, and this time it was Jefferson who danced in.

"Uncle Drayton wants everybody downstairs!" he sang out. "And I already know what it's about!"

"Well, bully for you," Polly said.

Jefferson stuck his tongue out at her, ignored his mother's scolding, and pranced back out. The rest of them followed in nervous silence. Austin tried to get next to Charlotte, but she waggled her shoulders away and hurried down ahead of him. If things had ever looked stormier, inside or out, he didn't know when.

Uncle Drayton had them assemble in the front sitting room,

where Josephine and Mousie were spreading out biscuits and pre-serves and tea, all of which only Jefferson attacked. Ria sat stiffly by the door.

Austin couldn't sit down. He stood behind the couch, where his mother perched on the edge of the seat and held Jefferson with a vice grip.

Uncle Drayton didn't even say good morning. He started right in.

"I have already spoken to young Corporal Wylie this morn-ing—before dawn."

That brought a smile to Polly's face.

"He is assistant to a colonel, and I trust his word. He says that only three of the ships President Lincoln has sent have been able to make it into the harbor."

"Then they *are* here!" Mother said. "We should get down to the harbor!"

"And be swept away in this storm," Aunt Olivia said. Then her eyes took on that maybe-that's-not-such-a-bad-idea look.

"No," Uncle Drayton said. "Even they are waiting at the mouth of the harbor for the storm to die down. And I have worse news."

The room seemed to come to attention. Even Jefferson stopped squirming.

"The Confederate cabinet has ordered Beauregard to fire on the fort if necessary to prevent its reinforcement."

"Then it's war," Austin said woodenly.

"Very probably."

"What's to be done?" Mother said. "Unless we get to one of those boats out in the harbor—"

"On a day like this? Sally, that would be suicide."

"Will this never end?" Aunt Olivia cried.

Sally Hutchinson put Jefferson to the side and stood up. Austin couldn't see her face, but he could see the sudden, steady straightness in her back. It made him listen hard.

"Olivia, whether I leave here today or live with you for the rest of our lives is the very least of your worries. You have no idea what is about to happen around you, do you?"

"Stop trying to frighten me, Sally Hutchinson!" Olivia cried. "You're trying to stir up trouble again, though heaven knows you've done enough. My eldest daughter is gone, my youngest daughter is likely to follow the same path, my husband is deathly ill, our most promising slave is about to be sold—and all because of you and your little Wesley-boy." She pointed a plump finger at Austin and held it there while her chins trembled.

It does sound like I've done a lot, Austin thought with a start. *And now, just one more thing.*

"But how can I?" he whispered.

He hadn't meant to say it out loud. But there was so much commotion in the room, it was obvious no one had heard him. Aunt Olivia was screaming gibberish, and Mousie was waving two handkerchiefs in her face. Uncle Drayton was yelling about everybody being quiet and no one was, least of all Jefferson, Tot, and Polly, who were all squalling. Sally Hutchinson calmly left the room with Ria behind her. The only person who even looked at Austin was Charlotte.

And she just looked terribly, terribly sad.

When she suddenly jumped out of her chair and ran from the sitting room, Austin went after her. She was only a few steps up when she looked down and saw him.

"All those things Mama said were true, Austin," she said with tears in her voice. "You did do all that, and I helped you. We had such good times together. Why did you have to spoil it now?"

Before he could answer—if he'd even known what to say— she disappeared up the elegant staircase. Austin sank down on the bottom step.

I spoiled it for nothing, he told himself. *I did it all for that one more thing, and now it isn't going to happen.*

And then came that thought again: *But at least you can try.*

He was no further along in figuring out what to do by late afternoon when the storm slackened off and there was a knock on the front door. Everyone in the family—except Henry-James—rushed to see who it was. Polly was the most delighted. It was young Corporal Wylie.

At least I get to see Polly make a fool of herself one more time, Austin thought from the staircase. *I wonder how many handkerchiefs she'll drop.*

He missed having Charlotte to roll his eyes at.

"Welcome, Corporal," Uncle Drayton said, extending his hand.

The rosy-cheeked young man, who Austin was sure didn't look much older than himself, shook Uncle Drayton's hand in return, but his eyes were searching the room. There was no mistaking it—they lit up when he saw Polly. She blushed and looked demurely down at her skirt.

Well, I'll be, Austin thought.

"General Beauregard is going to be true to his word, sir," the corporal finally said. "He'll fire on the fort if those ships make a move, and so far they haven't. The people are going so wild that he's ordered a parade through the streets tonight."

"Just what they need," Uncle Drayton said dryly. "An excuse to go even wilder."

"He thinks it will work off some of their energy," he said.

"Or get them even more bloodthirsty," Uncle Drayton said.

"Drayton, really!" Aunt Olivia said. "Such vulgar talk!"

What did he say that was so vulgar? Austin wanted to whisper to Charlotte.

"Will I see you all there, sir?" Corporal Wylie asked.

"Where, at the parade?" Uncle Drayton said.

Austin watched Polly. She had a "Please, Daddy!" on her lips, but she was holding it back admirably.

"I want no part in this foolishness," Uncle Drayton said. "I am against this war."

Wylie looked disappointed. Polly looked as if she were about to cry. Only Corporal Wylie's special look at her before he left brought the sparkle back into her eyes.

All afternoon, Polly begged her father to let her go to the parade with Tot, but he wouldn't hear of it. When the drums began to roll down at the park around the corner and the cannons started to rumble on their sling carts along the still-watery streets, Uncle Drayton pursed his lips and shook his head and let Polly cry.

"The child is miserable, Drayton," Aunt Olivia chided him. "Why can't at least one person in this house be happy?"

Drayton relented only a little. He said they could go up on the roof and watch from there.

There was a frenzied, almost hysterical kind of excitement in the air as they all headed for the rooftop. Mousie, Josephine, and Ria set up chairs, and Aunt Olivia insisted that they have cakes as well.

"This is not a picnic, Olivia," Uncle Drayton said.

She wiggled her chins and snapped at Josephine to bring on the treats.

Charlotte made it a point to get as far away from Austin as she could. Polly was busy searching for Wylie in the parade, with Tot's help, and his mother spent most of her time trying to keep Jefferson from hurtling off the roof.

Austin watched listlessly—and then suddenly he felt his eyes bulge.

There, in the crowd below, was Fitzgerald Kearney.

There was no mistaking him. He always walked as if life were an adventure. He was the rowdiest reveler in the throng.

"Fitz!" he cried.

And then he plastered both hands over his mouth and looked frantically at the group on the roof. No one even looked his way.

Trying to look as casual as he could, Austin strolled across the roof to the steps and slowly made his way down. As soon as he knew his head had disappeared from sight, he broke into a run.

For about two steps.

The stairs were still slippery from the rain, and as usual, his feet were uncooperative. He took a tumble to the bottom, landing in the hallway in front of the attic door with a resounding thud.

Holding his breath, he rolled into the dormer area and waited.

There was no change in the noise above him. No unusual silence or questioning voices. No one was coming to see what sack of potatoes had just been dropped off the staircase.

Austin scrambled up and went to the window and then rolled his eyes at himself. Fitz was on the other side. He'd have to go to a front window. The attic. But the key—

Austin gave a gasp and dug into the pocket of his jacket. It was still in there.

Fumbling with trembling fingers, he scooped it out and jiggled the lock open. He didn't even bother to lock it behind him as he hurried around the dark forms of crates and boxes toward Henry-James.

He wasn't there.

"Henry-James?" he whispered.

There was no answer.

Austin stooped to the floor and picked up the chain, but there was obviously no Henry-James on the end of it. He stood up and searched wildly with his eyes.

"Henry-James!" he dared to call out a little more urgently.

Still there was no answer. Only a sigh.

Squinting, Austin felt his way across the room. His foot caught on something, and he went sprawling. His hand, as he reached out to break his fall, hit something hard and thin.

It was the bar of a cage.

He knew it before he even got himself up to see.

Henry-James was in a cage—the very cage they'd thought to use to get food up to him. It was so small that the slave boy had to sit with his knees pulled up and his shoulders hunched over like a possum caught in a trap.

"Oh, no," Austin whispered. "Oh, Henry-James, no."

Henry-James said nothing. He stayed crouched with his back to Austin and his head between his knees.

"It's all right, Henry-James," Austin whispered. The squirrel had lodged itself in his throat again. "I'm going to get you out of here."

Henry-James didn't seem to hear. Austin raced to the window and pushed open the pane.

"Fitz!" he shouted. "Fitz, up here!"

He was nowhere in sight. The crowd was moving fast and had probably already taken him with it. Even so, Austin shouted again—and again. Until a voice behind him said, "Why are you calling Fitz, Austin? What do you want with him?"

If he could have squeezed himself through, Austin knew he would have jumped out the window so he wouldn't have to turn around and face Charlotte. There was no need to, however. She stomped over and grabbed his arm, pulling him back so that they were nose to nose.

"Answer me, Austin," she said. Her eyes held the Ravenal blaze.

"He's going to help me get Henry-James to freedom," he said.

In slow, determined moves, Charlotte began to shake her head.

"I know you're afraid he's going to go through all that terrible stuff I was telling you about," he said. "But it won't happen, Lottie, I know it! Kady is taking care of everything. She would never let him get hurt. She's worked hard to make all the right plans."

"No," Charlotte said. "You can't take him. You can't take him away!"

"Don't you want him to have a better life?" Austin said.

"He won't have one! He'll have to run all his life!"

"He'll be fine! He's smart. He can read and write. And he'll never be beaten again, Lottie—or put in a cage."

"He's never been put in a cage!" Lottie cried.

Austin didn't answer her. He just turned her around and pushed her toward the pen where Henry-James was crouched. If it was possible, he pulled himself into an even tighter ball.

There was stillness, the kind Austin was learning to notice—where the eerie quiet of before-the-storm set his heart to pounding. It was broken by the most tortured cry Austin had ever heard.

"Lottie, hush!" he whispered. "They'll hear you!"

Charlotte herself was beyond hearing. Bent in half, she backed away from the cage. Austin tried to grab her, if only to get his hand over her mouth. She wrenched away, knocking him backward, and hurled herself toward the door.

"Lottie, be quiet!" Austin hissed to her.

"I won't be quiet!" she cried. "I'll tell my father that you're trying to help Henry-James escape if I have to!"

"Come on, Lottie! Do you think Jesus wants him to be sold to people who won't love him the way you do? That's what's going to happen!"

"There's hate everywhere!" she said.

"What?"

"There's hate—and now I hate, too. I hate you, Austin!"

If she had plunged a knife into him, she couldn't have hurt him more. He stood rooted to the floor as she pushed open the door and disappeared.

"You gots to go after her, Massa Austin," said a voice from the cage.

It was the only thing that could have gotten Austin across the attic and back up onto the roof. His eyes darted from one person to another until he found Uncle Drayton. He was watching the parade, back ramrod straight. But there was no Lottie with him.

Austin didn't bother to try to escape notice this time. He raced to the second floor to Charlotte's room. Her door was locked, and he could hear her inside, sobbing in chokes that stabbed his heart.

"Lottie?" he called to her. "Lottie, I have to talk to you."

"Go away!"

"I will. And I'll never bother you again. You just have to promise that you won't tell your father. Promise, Lottie."

"I hate you!"

"I know. I hate me, too. But this is for Henry-James, not me. Will you do it for him?"

She stopped crying out loud, but there were no words. Austin squeezed his eyes shut and leaned his forehead against the door.

"Please, Lord, please just this one more thing. I know this has to be. Please, no matter who I have to be or how much they hate me. Please—"

"I won't tell."

Austin opened his eyes—and realized he'd prayed out loud.

"What did you say?" he whispered.

"I won't tell. Now go away."

He did. His heart stopped pounding. It slowed to a sad, sad rhythm.

✢ ✢ ✢

Chapter Fifteen

The parade went on far into the night. No one in the Ravenal house slept much, even after the soldiers and their cheering supporters went off to bed. Austin himself lay awake, trying not to feel abandoned in his storm, listening for a pebble on his window or a knock at the front door.

None came until dawn. Once again, it was Corporal Wylie.

This time Aunt Olivia insisted that they all sit down in the sitting room, and she called for biscuits and strawberries.

"I really do have to hurry, ma'am," young Wylie said to her. "I'm likely to see my first battle soon."

"What's happening?" Uncle Drayton said.

It took Corporal Wylie a moment to answer. His eyes were fixed on Polly, as if he were checking to be sure she was properly impressed. She was.

"Corporal?" Uncle Drayton said.

"Oh," he said. His already-rosy cheeks burned brighter. "General Beauregard has demanded that Major Anderson surrender Fort Sumter at once."

"No supplies got through, then," Mother said.

Corporal Wylie shook his head. "And that stubborn old coot out there says he'll only leave by April 15—due to lack of supplies—unless he gets other instructions from President Lincoln."

Austin remembered Major Anderson. He was a sad-eyed man who had shown nothing but kindness to the women and children on James Island last winter. He was far from being a stubborn old coot.

"General Beauregard is not going to wait until April 15, I can tell you that," Wylie said. Austin would have noticed the corporal's chest puffing out for Polly's benefit if his mind hadn't begun storming again.

War—before we can get away.

War—before I can get Henry-James to freedom.

War—before I can keep Uncle Drayton from selling him.

War—and Charlotte and I will be enemies.

Austin snorted to himself. *As if we aren't already. She said it. She hates me.*

Somehow that made the need to help Henry-James even stronger. It pushed him out of his chair and out of the sitting room. First things first—keep Uncle Drayton from going to the auction today.

For once, something went his way. Uncle Drayton was far too distracted by Corporal Wylie's news to even think about Henry-James. He shut himself up in his library. Aunt Olivia prepared for the evening's parade activities as if she were throwing a party. Sally Hutchinson sat in the sitting room and waited for word.

None came. The parade started at noon and went on all day. Austin went up on the roof again, pretending to watch the almost out-of-control crowd, but he was really searching for Fitz. He didn't appear.

Around eleven o'clock, Mother insisted that he go to bed. "You never know what tomorrow may bring," she said. Her face was strained. She hadn't looked that pale since Ria had nursed her back to health.

Austin didn't argue with her, but he couldn't fall asleep. He prayed, he thought, he ached. Sleep wouldn't come.

Around two o'clock, the crowd in the street finally thinned out, but the quiet was even more disturbing than the noise had been, and Austin couldn't lie still any longer. He got up, put on his jacket over his night clothes, and went back up to the roof.

The sky was velvet black and jeweled with stars.

How can the world still look so beautiful, Lord, when everything is so horrible? Austin thought.

"I see you've found my thinking place."

Austin looked up in surprise to see Uncle Drayton striding toward him in his silk robe. Austin hadn't seen him all day. In the pale light, he could see that his uncle's face was gray and his eyes were circled by dark rings.

"I wasn't really thinking," Austin said tightly. "I was praying."

"I think I knew that. I've tried to be a praying sort. I've never been very successful."

Austin didn't answer.

"Will you pray something for me?" Uncle Drayton said.

Austin felt his eyebrow twitch. "What?" he said.

"Don't worry, I think it's something you want, too. In fact, I know it is." Uncle Drayton sighed. "Pray to God that there will be no war—that this lunacy we've gotten ourselves into will cease before it even starts. You can pray for that, can't you?"

"Yes, sir," Austin said.

Uncle Drayton got quiet, as if he thought Austin might be praying right then and there.

They were still for a long time—until a sudden boom broke the night.

"Thunder?" Austin said.

Uncle Drayton stood up and pointed, shaking his head.

Even as he looked, Austin saw a ball of fire sail across the black sky.

"Cannon," Uncle Drayton said. "Right at Fort Sumter."

The words were barely out of his mouth when another shot was fired from a different direction.

"First one from James Island. Second one from Morris," he said.

Another fireball rocked the night, and then another. Austin craned his neck fearfully toward Fort Sumter.

"They aren't firing back," he said.

"Perhaps they're still praying what you're praying, Austin." Uncle Drayton narrowed his eyes at still another fireball flying above their heads. "But it doesn't seem as if God is listening."

The shells rained on as Austin and Uncle Drayton sat in silence. Toward morning the rest of the household began to appear, rubbing their eyes and asking sleepy questions.

"Has it begun?"

"Are we winning?"

"There is no winning in war!"

"Now we don't have to go! Now we don't have to go!"

That last comment, of course, came from Jefferson. Aunt Olivia turned on him with sleep-baggy eyes.

"Settle yourself down, young man!" she snapped. "Tot, do something with him!"

"Why is that Tot's job?" Polly said. "I'm as upset as he is—I need Tot! What if Corporal Wylie is wounded?"

"Why am I being spoken to in this manner?"

"Because you're acting foolish, Mama!"

"I will not—*what* are you doing, girl?"

Tot was suddenly standing between Polly and her mother. Austin was sure the look in her eyes was the same one Charlotte had seen the day Tot was grinding up poison mushrooms for Aunt Olivia's tea.

"What do you think you're doing?" Aunt Olivia said.

"She's protecting me, Mama," Polly cried.

"From what?"

"From *you!*"

"Quiet! Both of you!" Uncle Drayton shouted.

"We're having our own war right here on the roof," Austin muttered.

"Polly, take your slave out of my sight. She'll be the next to go if she's not careful."

Polly sent up a squall that out-burst the cannons. It was hard to tell who was ushering whom down the steps from the roof.

By then it was beginning to get light. *It must be seven o'clock*, Austin figured.

That was when it happened. From out in the harbor, a lone cannonball burned through the morning. Fort Sumter had finally returned fire.

"Now, then," Uncle Drayton said. "They're having their war."

No one else left the roof all day as the firing continued, back and forth—to a chorus of cheers from the whole city of Charleston. Josephine brought up breakfast. Only Sally Hutchinson went to wait again in the sitting room.

"I cannot sit and watch useless destruction," she said.

She was only gone a few minutes before Austin had an idea. It came from nowhere—but it felt right.

"I'm going to go check on her," he said to anyone who would listen. "She's upset."

Aunt Olivia sniffed.

Austin hurried down the steps, dug in his pocket for the key, and let himself into the attic.

"It's me, Henry-James," he whispered.

Henry-James was no longer curled up in a ball. He was waiting eagerly at the cage door, gripping its thin bars.

"The war done started, Massa Austin?" he asked.

"Yes," Austin said. "And I think this is our last chance to get you out of here." He examined the padlock on the cage and looked around the attic. "If I can get you out of the house, do you think you can get to Kady's on your own? There's so much confusion out there, nobody will even notice you."

"You done gone to all this trouble, Massa. I think I can at least do that."

Austin stopped in the middle of reaching for an old walking stick and looked at Henry-James.

"Can I ask one thing of you before you go?" he said.

"What you want, Massa Austin?"

"I want you to stop calling me master. You and I are equals, Henry-James."

In the dim, early morning light of the attic, a smile spread across Henry-James's face, revealing the wonderful gap between his two front teeth that Austin liked so much.

"Even if I don' get away," he said, "I's free from this minute on."

Austin returned the grin and then went back to examining the walking stick.

"What you gonna do with that, Mas—?" He stopped. "I mean, Austin?"

"I'm going to try to pry these bars apart enough for you to be able to reach your hand out and break this padlock. I know you're strong enough."

"That won't work," someone said.

Austin jumped. It was Charlotte.

"How do you keep getting in here?" he said—stupidly.

"You keep leaving the door unlocked behind you," she said. "Kady said you should never try to be a spy, and she was right. You need me to help you."

Austin exchanged glances with Henry-James.

"I thought you didn't want Henry-James to go," Austin said. "I thought you hated me."

"I changed my mind," she said. Then she shook her head. "No, you changed my mind. About both things. But we don't have time to talk about that. I think we should take him out, cage and all."

"What good will that do?" Austin said.

"We can carry him through town like we're going to the slave auction."

"But how are we going to get him out of the house?" Austin said.

She looked at the window. "We could try to lower him down."

"Somebody might see us!" Austin said.

"How about your mother's bedroom window? That's way in the back. All we have to do is get the cage to the second floor."

"And if someone catches us lugging this thing down the steps—*if* we can even do it?"

Charlotte broke into a surprising grin. "At least you admit it now, Austin," she said. "Now you're thinking."

He didn't understand, and he didn't have time to figure it out. He looked around the attic again.

"All right," he said. "We're playing a game."

Charlotte nodded slowly.

"We're pretending that you and I are elegant people of Charleston," he went on, "riding down the street in our carriage. . . ." As he talked, he gathered up several blankets and draped them over the cage. "Hop on," he said.

"Do we have horses?" she said. Her eyes were taking on the old pretend-game shine. "Jefferson?" But she immediately shook her head.

"Bogie," said a voice under the blanket.

Austin locked gazes with Charlotte. They both started to nod.

With everyone on the roof, it wasn't hard to get Bogie unchained from his stake in the garden. He was trembling from the sound of the cannon fire, but halfway up the first flight of the back stairs, he began to wag his tail and sniff the air.

"He already smells Henry-James," Charlotte said.

"Dogs have an amazing sense of smell," Austin said. "I've read about it—"

"Austin, not *now*," Charlotte said.

They could hardly keep Bogie from scratching right through the attic door, and once he realized Henry-James was under the blanket, there was no stopping him. There was nothing to do but take the drapes off and let Bogie lick Henry-James until Bogie stopped whining.

"I gots to say somethin'," Henry-James said.

His voice came out in a dull thud that stopped Austin's heart.

"What?" Charlotte asked.

"I can't go less'n I knows somebody gonna look after Bogie."

"Of course!" Austin said.

"It can't be you, Mas—I mean, Austin," Henry-James said. "You gots to escape your own self."

"I'll take care of him until you come back, Henry-James," Charlotte said.

Bogie looked from one of them to the other and then dug his face squarely into the front of Charlotte's dress. She buried her own face in the wrinkles of his head, and Austin knew she was hiding her tears.

He felt like crying, too, because they all knew Charlotte was wrong. If Henry-James got away, he was never coming back.

"All right, boy," he said. "Now it's time to go to work."

Bogie stood patiently while they found some old scarves and harnessed him to their "coach." Charlotte and Austin pushed it from behind all the way out the attic door and into the dark hall before they got on.

"Pull, Bogie!" Austin whispered to him.

Bogie tried, but the coach barely budged an inch.

"That's all right," Austin said. "We only need him if someone comes."

They hopped off and pushed the cage while Bogie pulled,

bumping it hideously down the steps to the second floor.

"Why do you say things like that, Austin?" Charlotte said. "You make them happen—here comes somebody now!"

"Just pretend we're playing a game," Austin said.

"No, they're coming!" Charlotte wheezed through her teeth. "I'm scared!"

"Your room!" Austin whispered.

"We'd have to go backward! Your mother's room—it's closer!"

Charlotte opened the door and pulled Bogie through. Then she came back and helped Austin push the cage from behind. A few seconds later, he closed the door.

"Well, well," Sally Hutchinson said. "I see you two have made up."

Austin jumped. His mother was sitting in a chair by the window, nodding at them.

Bogie wagged happily and slurped at her hand. She petted him absently as she examined Austin's and Charlotte's faces. Her eyes narrowed.

"All right, you two," she said, "what are you up to?"

"Playing," Charlotte said, voice as wobbly as her mother's chins.

Mother crossed to them and tapped the top of the cage. "And in here we have—"

Outside in the hall, footsteps drew nearer. They all held their breath as they passed.

"The next person might not go by," Mother said. "I think you'd better let me in on your secret."

Reluctantly, Charlotte pulled off the blankets. Bogie threw back his head and howled, and Austin dove for him and stuffed the dog's baggy face into his shirt.

Mother knelt down to look at Henry-James. Then she took the padlock in her hand.

"I think we need a hair pin," she said. She plucked one out of her tawny hair and bent to the lock. In a moment, it pulled easily open.

And not a moment too soon. More footsteps approached, this time up the steps.

"Come out of that hideous cage," Mother said to Henry-James. "And hide under the bed. You, too, Bogie."

"What about the cage?" Charlotte said.

"You mean our trunk?" Austin said.

He pulled the blankets back over it and slid it over to join the rest of their waiting baggage.

"Come in," Mother sang out to the knock on the door.

The door pushed slowly open, and a swollen-eyed, blotchy-faced Polly stuck her head in.

"Polly," Mother said. "Come in, you poor thing."

Any other time, Austin would have rolled his eyes at Charlotte. But there was something real about Polly's tears this time. She was hiccuping and blowing bubbles out of her nose, none of which was very romantic.

Polly went to Sally Hutchinson, wringing her hands and shaking her head.

"What's happened?" Mother said. "Has someone hurt you?"

"Tot," Polly said.

"Tot hurt you?"

"No!"

"Tot hurt somebody else?" Austin asked.

He heard Charlotte gasp. He knew she was thinking of mushrooms, too.

"No!" Polly sputtered. "Mama . . . she threw a tray at Tot . . . hit her . . . right in the head!"

"Oh, good heavens!" Mother cried. "Is she all right? Does she need Ria?"

Polly shook her head. "She has a big . . . lump. . . . She's hiding . . . under my bed."

There seemed to be a lot of that going on. Austin willed himself not to stare right at his mother's bed ruffle to see if any part of Henry-James or Bogie was sticking out.

"I have a pot of tea here," Mother said. "Come sit down and let's get you calmed—"

"No, Aunt Sally. I need . . . I need your help."

"Anything, you know that."

Polly nodded—and hiccuped—and then smeared her hand under her nose. Mother handed her a handkerchief.

But Polly waved it off and looked at her aunt through the slits her eyes had become.

"When Uncle Wesley sends for you," she said, "I want you to take Tot with you."

✟ ✟ ✟

Chapter Sixteen

ven the bed hangings seemed to be holding their breath. Austin, of course, was the first to get his bearings.

"Take Tot with us? Polly, you know we don't believe in slavery!"

His mother put her hand on his arm. "I don't think that's what Polly means, Austin."

Polly shook her head, the limp, lifeless curls barely moving. "I want her to be free. I want her to go to the North, where no one can ever hit her on the head or scream at her or threaten to sell her—ever, ever again!"

The words seemed to be pushed out by sobs, and Polly threw her hands over her face and flung herself face down onto the bed. Austin winced at the thought of Henry-James underneath.

Mother put her finger to her lips and climbed up beside Polly.

"Polly, love, I don't even know yet how the boys and I are going to get out of the South. Trying to take Tot with us would be dangerous for all of us. You don't want that, do you?"

"Yes!" Polly cried into the bed clothes. "Austin would make sure nothing happened to her. He's smart enough!"

Austin felt his mouth drop open.

"I'm sure Austin appreciates your confidence," Mother said. "But I just don't see how—"

"I do," Charlotte said.

They all looked at Lottie. Even Polly pulled her head up from the bed, dripping like a leaky bucket.

"There's another way Tot can go to freedom, Polly," Charlotte said. "She can go with Henry-James."

Austin's breath sliced through him like a butcher knife. It was too late to say it now, but the words "Lottie, you have an even bigger mouth than *I* do" burned on his lips.

Polly sat up and stared at her little sister. "You're letting Henry-James go?"

"Perhaps we should speak a bit more softly," Mother said.

Austin nodded and went to the door to peek out. It gave him a chance to rearrange his face. Of all the things that could have happened today, this would have been the last one he'd ever have expected.

And yet . . .

His thoughts began to teem as he quietly shut the door and turned around. This had possibilities. Very good possibilities.

"Do you have plans for Henry-James?" Polly said. "Can . . . this person . . . can he take Tot, too?"

"I don't know—" Mother started to say.

But Austin marched up to Polly, catching Charlotte's eye as he went. The way she was looking at him, he knew she would be right behind him.

"I think he'd be glad to," Austin said. "But you have to help, too."

"I'll do anything to get my girl out of here." She looked like she was going to start to cry again, so Austin rushed in with the plan that was still formulating in his mind.

"Do you know how to get in touch with Corporal Wylie?" Austin said.

Polly blinked—but only for a moment. Then her face grew pink and she said, "As a matter of fact, I do."

Austin heard Charlotte sniff, but he grabbed Polly by the wrist and pulled her off the bed. "He's a fighting man now. He needs a couple of valets—soldiers often have them—I read about that. Get a message to him. Tell him you have two Negroes for him, but he has to give you uniforms for them, *with* a kepi."

Although she looked a little dazed, Polly nodded.

"And tell him in the message that *you* will bring the boys to *him*, all right?"

"The boys? But what about Tot?"

Austin grinned. "She's one of the boys."

"But how—?"

"Just do that much," Austin said. "And don't tell Tot yet what you're doing. She'll be better off not knowing."

He wasn't sure Polly could hold any more in her head right now, and besides, the plan was still taking shape. It was coming from that sure, strong place.

"All right," Polly said. She tried to straighten her narrow shoulders, but they collapsed. "I don't know if I can do this."

"Of course you can," Mother said.

"But I'm not brave enough—not like those women in the books who can do all sorts of noble things."

"Polly, don't be a goose," Charlotte said. "You are brave. It takes a lot of courage to let your best friend go."

Austin took a giant breath. If that could happen, then just about anything was possible.

Jesus was in the middle of this storm after all.

Polly hurried out, calling for Tot. Austin dropped to his knees and lifted up the bed ruffle. Two pairs of eyes looked out at him.

"Come on out, boys," Austin said. "We have plans to make."

The firing of cannons went on all day. Uncle Drayton certainly never thought to check on the slave boy in the attic. Polly went into the kitchen and told Josephine that Tot would take the food up to him—and because it was Polly, Josephine never suspected a thing. She was glad to let her, in fact. After all her trips to the roof with trays and teapots, Josephine was weary of stairs.

Austin made another trip up to the roof to make sure that neither Uncle Drayton nor Aunt Olivia suspected anything. He asked questions about the artillery fire—which he already knew the answers to—until Uncle Drayton sighed wearily and said, "Suppose you go down and see how Josephine is coming along with supper?"

"Of course," Austin said.

He gave Josephine the benefit of the doubt, however, and raced back to his mother's room. To his delight, Henry-James was already decked out in a gray private's uniform.

"Toby told Tot that the Negroes aren't supposed to have uniforms, but since it's General Beauregard's unit, he thought it would be proper."

"Who's Toby?" Austin said.

"Corporal Wylie, silly!" Polly said.

When did they get on a first-name basis? Austin thought. Polly was turning out to be a lot more sly than he'd suspected.

Austin held up the other uniform. It was much wider than Henry-James's and should do quite nicely for Tot.

"All right," he said. "Now for—"

"Austin, love," Mother said briskly. "Suppose you and Charlotte go up and check on Jefferson, all right?"

"Mother!" Austin said. "There are things to do!"

"I know," she said. "And that is one of them. Scoot."

Austin was still grumbling as he and Charlotte made their way up to the roof.

"I don't know what that was all about," Austin said.

"I do," Charlotte said. "You have a lot of gifts, Austin, but saying the right thing at the right time isn't one of them."

"Oh," Austin said.

"But don't let it worry you," Charlotte said. "I never know what to say either."

"You did a good job with Polly," he said.

"I just know how she feels," Charlotte said. "Can we talk about something else, Austin?"

Austin was more than willing.

When they got back to Mother's room an hour later, after stuffing Jefferson with gingersnaps and sacrificing some of their toys for him to play with, Tot, too, was dressed in full regalia.

Austin inspected her. The jacket gaped a little across the belly and the pants had to be rolled up at the ankles, but with the kepi over her short, stubby braids, she made a passable soldier.

"Did you tell her?" he heard Charlotte whisper to Polly.

Austin could have answered that question. Tot looked like she was standing up in her sleep, and Polly's eyes were red and swollen again.

She nodded.

"You look perfect, Tot," Austin said.

Bogie licked her hand, and Henry-James nodded his approval.

"Tell me again why I gots to wear this," Tot said.

Austin's head snapped toward Polly, who sighed.

"Because I want you to have a better life," she said.

"You goin' with me?" Tot said.

Polly shook her head.

"Then I don't wanna go, Miz Polly!"

Her voice wound up so high that Bogie whined and went to the floor, where he covered his ears with his paws.

"You have to," Polly said. "I'm ordering you."

"I always done everything you tol' me, Miz Polly!" Tot cried. "But I can't do this thing. I do anything but this thing!"

For a minute, Austin thought Polly was going to give in. But Henry-James cleared his throat.

"Tot, you gots to listen to me," he said.

Tot looked at him as if she'd never seen him before.

"You been hearin' all them cannons goin' off?"

Tot nodded. " 'Bout scared me to death!"

"That means they's a war goin' on," Henry-James said. "It's twixt the North and the South."

She nodded, although Austin wasn't convinced she understood a word of it.

"If the North whups, you be free as Marse Drayton. You can come back here then and take right up with Miz Polly again." His eyes darkened. "But if'n the South whups, you gonna be a slave all your days—and Marse Drayton or Miz Livvy could sell you away from Miz Polly at the drop of a hat."

"No!" Tot cried.

" 'Zactly," Henry-James said. "That's why you gots to go North. That way, if'n the South whups, at least you's where you can decide where you wants to be."

"With Miz Polly," Tot said.

"And that's the way it will be," Polly said. She straightened her shoulders, and this time they didn't give. "I will come to the North and live. I don't want to live in a place where people can't decide for themselves! I could come live with you, couldn't I, Aunt Sally?"

Mother looked so stunned that Austin was surprised she was able to nod her head.

But that was all he needed to hear. There was no doubt about it. Jesus was in this.

Slowly, Tot nodded her head. Polly threw her arms around her thick neck, and the two of them bawled. Austin wriggled his shoulders uncomfortably.

"It's time to go," he said.

Polly pulled away and went to the table to pick up two sheets of paper.

"Here are your 'orders'," she said. "They say that you are reporting to Corporal Wylie. Show them to anyone who stops you."

"But you know where you're really going, Henry-James," Austin said.

Henry-James nodded.

"Why won't you tell me where that is?" Polly said.

"It's safer for you if you don't know," Mother said. "Just believe me, it's safer."

While Mother comforted Polly, Austin pulled Henry-James aside.

"You shouldn't have any trouble until you get out to where the tracks run parallel—that's where I ran into the dogs."

"That's why we gots Bogie," Henry-James said. "He can lead any pack o' dogs on a chase."

"Let's just hope he doesn't have to," Austin said.

"It's getting dark," Mother said. "It's time."

Heads nodded, but faces silently cried, "No! No, this is too hard!"

Austin tried to keep his mind on the plan—so his voice wouldn't waver.

"All right, this is going to be the hardest part," he said. "Charlotte and Polly are going to make sure everyone is occupied while you go out the back and through the garden. I'll be keeping watch from the back door."

"Remember," Charlotte said, "if you get down real low, you can slide under the hedge if you have to."

Tot nodded. "I done that before. Back at Canaan Grove."

"We know," Austin said. "Then when you're on Church Street, just walk like you're right where you're supposed to be, doing just what you're supposed to be doing."

The room got still. There was nothing else to say, except goodbye. And that no one seemed to be able to say.

"Where on earth *is* everyone?" a shrill voice called.

Every eye in Sally Hutchinson's room bulged.

"There is a meal waiting to be eaten on the roof! Does everyone need a written invitation?"

"Now," Mother said.

Mouths pasted into thin lines, they all moved. Walking as if he were in a dream, Austin went to the second-floor sitting room where they'd left Jefferson playing. He pictured his mother, Charlotte, and Polly going to the roof—Henry-James, Tot, and Bogie slipping down the back stairs. He hadn't counted on this little detour, but if he could just get Jefferson to the roof, he'd still have time to get down to the back door and make sure the fugitives got away safely.

His heart sank, however, when he reached the sitting room and Jefferson was nowhere to be found.

Heart pounding, he took the stairs three at a stride to the roof. Aunt Olivia had a blanket spread out and everyone was sitting on it, surveying a banquet spread. Jefferson wasn't among them.

Please, Lord, don't let him be in the garden. Please!

Not even trying to be quiet, he galloped down the back steps, tripping and stumbling. Before he even got the back door open, his heart fell completely to his knees. He could hear Jefferson's voice.

"But I want to play this game, too!" he was wailing. "I want a uniform like yours!"

Austin bolted out the door, in time to see Henry-James crouching to a squat in front of Jefferson. Austin ran toward them. In spite of what his mother had once told him, it might be time to gag his little brother after all.

"Jefferson, get up on the roof!" Austin said. "Supper's waiting!"

"I don't want supper! I want to play this soldier game! I hate you all—no one ever plays anymore!"

With that, Jefferson folded like a fireplace screen onto the ground and sobbed. Charlotte had been right. There was nothing but hate here anymore.

Austin reached down to pick him up and carry him screaming into the house, where he would threaten him to within an inch of his life if he breathed a word about seeing Henry-James in a uniform.

But Henry-James himself put up a hand to Austin and pulled Jefferson onto his knee.

"All right," he said. "You can play, Massa Jefferson. But you can't have a uniform like mine 'cause it seems to me that you and Massa Austin gots to be the Union soldiers, and me and Tot's got to be the Southrons."

"Confederates," Jefferson said.

"That's right," Austin said.

Jefferson smeared the tears off with the back of his hand.

"And since we're in enemy territory," Austin said, "we have to go into hiding. So you and I have to go into the storage shed and hide—while these two try to find us."

A bubbling giggle came out of Jefferson. It was the first one Austin had heard in weeks.

"Come on," Austin said. He grabbed Jefferson's hand. "I'll be Corporal Hutchinson and you can be . . . General Shrimp."

"General *Shrimp*!" Jefferson cried.

But he giggled all the way to the storage shed.

As they pushed open the door, Austin threw one more look over his shoulder. Henry-James and Tot were already running for the hedge.

Go with them, Jesus, Austin prayed.

Jefferson crouched down in the dark and waited for the Confederates to find them. Austin felt his way over old wheels and broken buckets to the dirt-covered window in the back of the shed. He wiped off the inside dirt with his hand and peered through the still-dusty glass.

It was getting so dark outside that it was even harder to see, but he could make out two forms scrambling under the hedge that bordered the Ravenals' property in back.

They're making it! he thought. And for the first time, it seemed real. Henry-James and Tot were leaving. And they weren't ever coming back.

Excitement and sadness tangled in his chest like two cats fighting. Austin tried to think of what to do next, of how to calm it all down. The thing to do was to figure out how to keep Jefferson from blabbering.

And then his mind *and* his heart *and* his breathing stopped. There was another form on the other side of the hedge, standing up. An older form—not Henry-James or Tot. Austin pressed his face against the glass. It looked like a soldier in a kepi.

And he was taking Henry-James and Tot by the arm—and dragging them off.

✝ ❖ ✝

ustin chomped down on his lip to keep from screaming, "Show him the papers, Henry-James! The papers!"

But he forced himself to be still, to breathe, to believe that Henry-James would remember everything he was supposed to do.

Still, it didn't look as if Henry-James were showing the man anything. Austin had to know.

"Stay here," he whispered to Jefferson. "I'm going to go out and reconnoiter."

"What's that?"

"It's an important military word," Austin said. "I'll teach it to you when I come back."

Jefferson nodded happily. Austin slipped out the door—and bolted it behind him.

"Sorry, shrimp," he whispered. "I'll make it up to you."

Flattening himself against the side of the shed, Austin crept to the back.

Please don't let me be a weakling, he prayed.

Taking one careful step at a time, he kept moving until he could catch a voice beyond the hedge. It wasn't Henry-James or Tot. He held his breath to listen.

159

"I've been watchin' this house, thinkin' I'd see my chance," the voice said. "But I didn't know there would be two of you."

Fear clutched at Austin, and yet even as his heart slammed, he realized there was something familiar about that voice. It had an Irish lilt.

"Fitz!" he hissed.

There was a short silence, and then came a chuckle.

"Austin, my boy!" Fitzgerald Kearney whispered back. "Come show yourself!"

With legs soft as sponge cake, Austin crossed to the hedge. Fitz stood with an arm around each slave's shoulder.

"I've been waiting for this opportunity for days," he said. "Kady said you'd come through—she never doubted it for a minute."

"I've never been so happy to see anyone!" Austin said.

"I'd love to stay and chat about it, but we have work to do, these two and I."

Just then, there was a squall from the direction of the shed.

"And it sounds like you do, too. Here—" He reached down to his waist and deftly pulled off his red satin sash. "I don't care much for all these fancy trimmin's on a soldier's uniform," he said. "Give this to the little one."

"Shall I gag him with it?" Austin said.

"In a manner of speaking," Fitz said.

With that, he winked and squeezed the shoulders of his new traveling companions. "Shall we?" he said.

There was another squeal from the shed, and Austin ran for it.

Behind him, a voice said, "Austin?"

Austin stopped and looked back. Fitz and Tot had disappeared beyond the hedge, but Henry-James still stood there, his eyes wide. He ran his tongue into the gap between his two front teeth—almost like a little boy. Austin felt his throat getting tight.

"Run, Henry-James," he said, "before somebody sees you."

But Henry-James didn't run. He stood dead-still and looked hard at Austin, as if he were trying to memorize his face.

"I gots to say, Austin, I ain't never gonna forget you."

"You won't have to!" Austin said. "We're going to see each other again someday."

But he knew it wasn't true, and so did Henry-James. The sadness in his eyes said it for both of them.

"I ain't never gonna forget you," Henry-James said again, " 'cause you the best man I knows."

Just then, Fitz's voice hissed playfully from beyond the hedge. "Let's move on, soldier."

Henry-James nodded. Then with one last look at Austin, he was gone.

"Good-bye, Henry-James," Austin whispered.

It was a long night for Austin. There was Jefferson to bribe. The Secret Sash worked wonders.

And there was Tot's absence to explain to Aunt Olivia, although Polly took care of that. She shut herself in her room, and everyone assumed Tot was in there, too.

And there was Charlotte to comfort. She was trying to be brave, Austin could see that, but more than once during the evening, her eyes overflowed and she ran off to hide so no one would see her cry.

Sleep was out of the question. Austin imagined every noise was some Fire Eater dragging Henry-James and Tot back to the townhouse, or Uncle Drayton going up to the attic to discover his body slave gone. He did go to sleep before dawn, only to be awakened by voices across the hall. He got up on one elbow and listened through a sleepy stupor. Uncle Drayton's voice pulled him straight up in the bed.

"They've been at it for 34 hours," Uncle Drayton was saying.

"I've already been to the Market—the word is that Fort Sumter is in ruins."

Austin went out into the hall to hear more.

"What does all of that mean, Drayton?" his mother said. "Tell me straight out."

"Major Anderson has agreed to surrender," Uncle Drayton said. "We've won this round."

The words were barely out of his mouth when there was a pounding on the front door below. Austin didn't bother to put on his clothes. He was the first one down to fling the door open.

Lawson Chesnut, Roger Pryor, and Virgil Rhett stood before him.

"You're still here?" Lawson Chesnut wheezed.

"You won't be for long!" Virgil Rhett's eyebrows nearly crossed each other.

"What is this?" Uncle Drayton said from the stairs. His long legs took the staircase in what seemed like one step. He pushed Austin behind him and stood, hands on hips, in front of the Fire Eaters. Austin peeked around him.

"Like it or not, Ravenal," Roger Pryor said through his nose, "the war is on. It's practically won!"

"So it would seem," Uncle Drayton said tightly.

"It's time you proved your loyalty to the Confederacy," Chesnut said. He tugged importantly at his waistcoat, which, Austin noticed, was covered in miniature Confederate flag pins.

"I am prepared to put on a uniform," Uncle Drayton said. "If that's what you mean."

"Glad to hear it," Chesnut said.

But Roger Pryor scowled at him, and at Uncle Drayton. The hands at his sides, Austin could see, were itching to be used.

"There's one more thing you have to do first, Ravenal," he said. He gave his head a jerk. "You have to hand over the Yankees living in your house!"

"To whom?" Uncle Drayton said.

"To us!"

It was as if they had all spoken together. It was the loudest blast of hatred Austin had heard yet.

Roger Pryor took a step forward. Uncle Drayton took one, too, backing Pryor into a startled Lawson Chesnut.

"Now see here, Ravenal," Chesnut said. "There's no use in your forcing us out of here—we have the law on our side now. The Confederate law!"

"Really?" Uncle Drayton said. "May I see your papers?"

"What papers?" Pryor growled.

Virgil Rhett scowled fiercely, and Chesnut gasped.

"The official papers demanding the release of Sally Hutchinson and her sons into your custody," Uncle Drayton said. "Come now, are we some kind of uncivilized government, or do we have a proper—"

"We'll get you your papers, Ravenal!" Roger Pryor cried. His nose seemed to pull itself into an angry point. "And then we're taking your sister and her sons away!"

He shoved back between the other two and stomped toward their waiting buggy. Virgil Rhett went after him, and Chesnut followed. But he turned and waggled a fat finger at Uncle Drayton. "Don't say we haven't warned you time and time again."

Uncle Drayton slammed the door on him.

"Will they get papers, Drayton?" Mother said from the stairs. She had one hand holding her robe shut and the other clutching Jefferson to her side.

"I would say within the hour," Uncle Drayton said.

It may have been the first time Austin had ever seen his mother panic. Her face drained of color, and she let go of her gown and gripped the banister. Ria and Polly rushed down the stairs and caught hold of her.

Aunt Olivia bustled in from the sitting room, already dressed as if she were going coaching. She was tying her bonnet under her chin.

"What on earth was that all about?" she said.

"Fire Eaters," Uncle Drayton said.

"I don't think you can continue to call them that, Drayton," she said. "We're all one now. Most of us."

Her eyes flitted up to her sister-in-law. Austin bit down hard on his lip.

Aunt Olivia looped her hands around Uncle Drayton's arm. "Come on, Drayton," she said. "If we don't start off, we'll miss the festivities."

"What festivities?" Polly said.

"The surrender!" she said. "We're going out in the boat to watch."

"There has been a change of plans," Uncle Drayton said.

Aunt Olivia pulled her hands away, and the chins began to vibrate.

"What on earth for?" she said.

"I must tend to Sally."

"Sally! Sally! Sally! It's always Sally! I am sick to death with this."

"Then go on your own!" Uncle Drayton snapped. "Go with Mary Chesnut or someone else! I don't care!"

Aunt Olivia drew herself up and tucked in her neck until a fourth chin appeared. "Very well, then," she said primly. "Polly, get Tot. We are leaving."

"I don't want to go, Mama," Polly said.

Every eye made its way up the steps. Austin thought Aunt Olivia was going to choke.

"Get your hat and jacket, Polly," Aunt Olivia said. "We are going."

"Do I have to, Daddy?" Polly said.

Uncle Drayton put his hands to his head and closed his eyes.

"Do what you will, both of you," he said. "I no longer have time for these silly—"

"Say no more. Say nothing more to me!" Aunt Olivia said. "Mousie!"

The tiny slave woman appeared out of the hall shadows.

"Come, we are going," Aunt Olivia said.

And without a wave, without a good-bye, without so much as a final sniff, she took herself out the front door with Mousie skittering after her. The door slammed behind her—and suddenly there was a lot less hate in the house.

Uncle Drayton looked up at Mother. "I must find a way to get you out of here before they return. Make no mistake about it, Sally, this is slipping right out of my hands."

Austin stared at him. There were tears—there were actually tears making Uncle Drayton's voice shake. It sounded like hopelessness.

Austin found himself shaking his head.

"We don't have to give up," he said. "We know someone who can help us."

Mother's eyebrows furrowed, and then they smoothed. Charlotte, who was peeking down from the curve in the staircase, nodded, and so did Polly. Jefferson busied himself with his sash.

"Who?" Uncle Drayton said.

"It's better that you don't know," Mother said.

"Can you take us in a carriage as far as Moultrie Street?" Austin said.

"I can," Uncle Drayton said. "But if you're seen . . . everyone knows who you are."

"They won't see us. We'll be hiding."

"A simple search will—"

"Austin will think of something, Daddy," Polly said. "He always does."

"Charlotte should ride ahead and tell . . . the people that we're coming so arrangements can be made," Austin said. "She can outride just about anybody."

Charlotte nodded and scampered off before Uncle Drayton could argue.

"Get ready, then," he said to the rest of them. "I'll have to drive the carriage myself. No, Ria—" He reached into his pocket and pulled out a key. "Go and bring Henry-James down. He can drive us."

Ria was the only one who nodded. Everyone else, except Jefferson, turned to stone.

There was nothing that could be done. Even Austin couldn't think of way to stop the disaster.

Uncle Drayton handed Ria the key, and she made her way stiffly up the stairs.

"Please," Uncle Drayton said to the rest of them. "Go and get ready."

It was an ashen-faced group that met in Mother's room. The fears were spoken the minute the door was closed.

"He's going to find out."

"What if those Negro-tracking dogs come after us when we get out of the carriage?"

"Where will we go once we've gotten to Kady's?"

"One thing is for sure," Austin said. "We have to get out of here now, or there will be no leaving at all."

It was as if something else had taken over in him. There was no voice. There was only a feeling.

"Get dressed," Mother said. "Be back here in 10 minutes."

It didn't take 10 minutes for Ria to come back from the attic. Austin was pulling on his shoes when he heard her push open his mother's door. Carrying one shoe, he hurried across the hall.

Ria was standing like a wooden pole just inside the door, her back to Austin.

"Where is he, Miz Sally?" she said. "Where is my boy?"

Austin could see his mother's face, as sad as any sight he'd seen in the past 24 hours. She couldn't seem to get her mouth to open.

"He's free," Austin whispered.

Ria didn't turn around. She only stood there for a time—an endless time.

And then she nodded and moved into the room. Austin hurried in after her and closed the door.

"What we gonna tell Marse Drayton?" she asked.

Mother shook her head, but Austin came around to stand in front of Ria. "The truth," he said. "Tell him Henry-James is gone."

Austin's mother opened her mouth as if to protest, but her eyes took on a glimmer.

"He's right, Ria," she said. "There is no sense in anything else. Everything has changed now. From this time on, everything is going to be different, and Drayton knows that."

"He gonna hunt him down," Ria said.

"He'll never find him if he tries," Austin said. "I promise you that."

The pinch on her face let go, for just a minute. "I sets a lot of store by that, Massa Austin," she said.

"Just call me Austin," he said. "From now on."

"Where is that boy?" Uncle Drayton called from below. "Where is the carriage?"

Mother made herself tall and hurried out into the hall. "Henry-James seems to have disappeared, Drayton," she said. "You'll have to drive the carriage yourself. We'll meet you in the stable."

And so it was done. After all the planning and the sneaking and the hiding, it was done. With the truth.

For a frightening second, Austin watched Uncle Drayton's eyes flare like a pair of torches. He tried not to cringe as he waited for the torrent of words to spew out.

But they didn't come.

Uncle Drayton drew himself up, tall and straight as a pole, and tightened his face.

"I see," he said. The flare snuffed out of his eyes, and he looked at Austin's mother. "I'll drive you, but we must move quickly."

Then with his usual southern-gentlemanly calm, he turned on his heel and took the steps two at a time.

Mother didn't even flinch. She took hold of Jefferson and talked to him in a fierce, low voice as she moved him down the back stairs.

Ria followed, her face tight and wooden.

Polly came out of her room with a cloth bag in her hand.

"I wanted to ask you something, Boston," she said. "I had an idea."

"What?" Austin said. He was still reeling.

"This is crushed eggshells," she said. "Suppose I powder my face with these so I look sickly. That way if anyone stops us, I can say Daddy is taking me to a doctor."

Slowly, Austin's mouth formed a grin. "I wish you'd been in on more of our plans," he said. "You're good at this."

"It wasn't the way I thought I was supposed to turn out," she said.

"I think it's the way God wants you, though," Austin said.

To his surprise, she nodded. And then she began to powder.

Uncle Drayton had the horse hitched up and the carriage ready. He stood at its door with a pile of blankets. "Under the seats, I think," he said. "Put these over yourselves." He looked at Ria. "If those miserable men should return before I get back, you tell them I've given them their wish. The Yankees are gone."

The minute Uncle Drayton climbed up into the driver's seat, Sally Hutchinson burst into tears. Austin looked up from trying to shove Jefferson under the seat. She put her arms around Ria, and they cried together. It made his insides ache, made him think a sad thought he couldn't push aside with any more plans.

They're friends, just like Charlotte and me. And they're never going to see each other again.

He comforted himself with only one thing—he would still see Charlotte when they got to Kady's. He could at least say good-bye.

With everyone in, the carriage lurched and their journey began. Polly sat above them on the seat, wrapped in a blanket and already playing the part of the invalid.

"We're on our way," she whispered to them. "I'll warn you if anything bad happens."

And then she gasped.

"What is it?" Austin hissed to her.

"Oh, dear. Oh, my."

"*Polly,* what is it?"

"It's a soldier, Austin," Polly said in a strangled voice. "He's stopping us right at the end of the drive!"

✦-✦-✦

Chapter Eighteen

ustin started to scramble out from under the blanket, but
Polly kicked him back. He heard her catching her breath.
"Don't—he'll see you!" she whispered. "I'm watch-
ing. He's talking to Daddy. I can't see his face, but I know it isn't
Corporal Wylie."

"That's good," Austin whispered. "He's probably wondering
where his Negroes are!"

"Is he wearing a red sash like mine?" Jefferson whispered.

"No, it's a dirty uniform," Polly said. "And he has his hat
pulled down over his eyes. This is not a handsome soldier—"

"Forget that!" Austin hissed to her, although at least that told
him it wasn't Fitz. "What is he doing?"

"He's talking to Daddy."

The carriage rocked to one side, and Polly gave a tiny squeal.

"What?" Austin said.

"Polly, please, we're dying of fright here," Mother said.

"I'm not!" Jefferson whispered.

"He's gotten onto the carriage with Daddy," Polly said. "We're
driving off with him in the seat next to Daddy!"

"This is not good," Mother said. "Not good at all."

"Is he taking us where the other soldiers are?" Jefferson said.

"Maybe that's where Tot and Henry-James went."

Austin grasped for anything to stop the pounding in his chest. *I know You're there, Lord*, he prayed desperately. *I know it's going to be all right. I can feel it—but I wish You'd show me how!*

"We're heading up the Battery," Polly said. "Just like we planned. I can't see what is happening up in the driver's seat, but we're passing the Roper House, the Alston place—"

They were going the best way to get to Kady's without being seen by many people. Even without Polly's commentary, Austin could hear that the wharves were to their right. They were on East Bay and quickly leaving the sounds of the marketplace and the shipyards behind.

"Tell us when we get to the railroad tracks!" Austin whispered.

"But what about when we get to Moultrie Street?" Mother said. "How is Drayton going to get us out of here without that soldier seeing us?"

"Maybe we're going to drop him off along the way," Austin said. That seemed like something Jesus would think of. He felt calm again. He closed his eyes and breathed deep.

A train whistle suddenly worked its way into his thoughts.

"Train," he whispered.

"Yes, and soldiers waving to us from the depot," Polly said. "We're stopping!"

"Jefferson," Austin heard his mother say through her teeth, "don't make a sound."

There was a muffled noise next to him. Unless he missed his guess, Austin's mouth.

The carriage rolled slowly to a stop. Austin could feel everyone stiffening in fear. But he only waited. There was something very strong, very sure about all this.

Above him, he could hear Polly opening the carriage window. Snippets of conversation drifted in.

"Passengers to go aboard?"

"No."

"Lucky for you."

"Searching everyone at this depot—"

"Catching miserable Yankees—"

"Don't you talk, soldier?"

Something about that pricked up Austin's ears. *"Don't you talk, soldier?"*

Uncle Drayton said, "Taking this soldier to a doctor . . . lost his voice in the yelling."

"That was quite a night!"

The carriage rocked back, then forward—and they were back on their way.

"Polly!" Austin whispered to her.

"What?"

"Wasn't that soldier talking when he got on our carriage at the house?"

"Yes!"

"Then why can't he talk now?"

Polly didn't answer. She didn't have to.

That isn't even a soldier, Austin thought.

And somehow, it was a hopeful thought.

"This is a wretched neighborhood," Polly whispered when they'd ridden on for a while. "Mama has never let me come this far north. We're stopping!"

The carriage indeed rocked to a halt. Jefferson began to wiggle.

"Just a minute!" Austin whispered to him. "Just another minute—and then we're going to run!"

"I want to run now!"

"Hush, Jefferson!" Polly whispered. "The soldier is coming!" She ended with a squeal.

There was a soft thud, and Austin guessed she was prostrating herself on the seat and giving her best imitation of a patient with pneumonia.

"Now!" Jefferson said—out loud.

He scrambled out from under the seat. Austin heard the carriage door open.

"Please!" Polly moaned. "I'm dying. Please, let my father take me to a—"

"Father!" Jefferson cried. "I didn't know you were a soldier, Father!"

Austin banged his head into his mother's getting out from under the seat.

"Wesley!" she cried.

Austin could only stare. It was indeed his father, standing at the door of the carriage, smiling at them from under the brim of a Confederate kepi.

"I'm no soldier, Jefferson," he said. "In fact, I can't *wait* to get this uniform off!"

"Not yet, Wesley," Uncle Drayton said behind him. "This is a good disguise."

No one was listening to him. Mother fell into Austin's father's arms and went limp. Jefferson crawled up onto his shoulders. Austin watched . . . and waited for his mind to catch up.

Blankly, he turned to Polly and said, "It's my father."

"I know," Polly said. She actually looked a little disappointed. Her act had been so good, and it had been wasted on Uncle Wesley.

"Austin, is that you?" Father said.

Austin nodded.

Father shook his head. "I would never have recognized you, son. You've grown into quite a man."

Austin didn't digest that. Somehow he could only watch as his father stood there next to Uncle Drayton, looking strong and sure.

"Hush!" Uncle Drayton said suddenly.

Austin leaned toward the door. He heard what Uncle Drayton must have. It was the faraway barking of dogs.

"We have go—now!" Austin said.

His father grabbed Jefferson's legs with one hand, securing him to his shoulders, and took Mother by the arm with his free arm.

"Can you keep up, Austin?" he said.

"Keep up?" Uncle Drayton said. "I think you'd do well to let him lead the way, Wesley."

The dogs were drawing closer. Austin jumped out of the carriage and looked around to get his bearings. The dogs were coming from the direction of town. At least they wouldn't run into them—but could they outrun them?

"Go!" Uncle Drayton said.

"Drayton—" his mother said.

Uncle Drayton cut her off with a thrust of his hand. "No good-byes, sweet potato pie. Just go. I'll head off anyone I can. Go!"

"Come on, Father, this way."

With the thoughts teeming again in his head, Austin headed across the lonely stretch of land.

Don't go through the stand of trees—stay away from the bushes. That's where the soldiers like to hide.

Go where the dogs can't track you.

Of course.

Austin veered sharply toward the other set of railroad tracks with his parents and Jefferson behind him. Moultrie Street was just on the other side, and as much as it had been raining, there was sure to be—

And there was. A gushy stream of rainwater still lay in the gully along the rise of the tracks.

"Walk in the water!" he whispered hoarsely to them as they

picked their way as quickly as they could across the railroad tracks.

No one said a word, but he could hear them splashing softly behind him.

The dogs can't smell us, Austin thought. *If we can only get away before they hear us.*

"Thank the Lord—a train," his father whispered.

Austin had to strain to hear the whistle, but sure enough, it was there in the distance.

"Crouch down!" Wesley Hutchinson ordered.

Austin bent low and moved faster. The train whistle grew louder, nearer, to cover their sounds. But so did the barking of the dogs.

"Just a little farther!" Austin hissed over his shoulder.

Unfortunately, they had to make a left turn to head down the little dirt road that led to Kady's cabin. That meant coming out of the water and providing a trail for the dogs.

The train came around the bend and thundered into view.

"Run!" Austin shouted. "That way!"

The clatter of the wheels, the blasting of the steam from the locomotive smothered his cries as the Hutchinsons splashed out of their stream and hooked left, making for the road that Austin could see now.

But coming at them from behind, yelping in piteous desperation, was the pack of dogs.

Austin kept running, his mind racing ahead of him.

It can't be over. I know it isn't over.

The barking went on—one howl rising above the others. One loud baying . . . that was coming from the other direction.

Even as Austin turned his head, a flash of flopping ears and flying skin went past him. Bogie was headed straight for the dog pack.

Every canine nose was suddenly pointed toward the bounding

bloodhound. Every ear seemed to stand up like a snail's antenna. With one veer, Bogie turned the entire pack around. All Austin could see were tails.

"Where on earth did that come from?" Father said.

"That was Bogie!" Jefferson cried. His voice was heading up into dangerous scream-territory. "Get Bogie, Austin!" he shouted. "They're going to kill him!"

With a mighty kicking of legs and flailing of arms, Jefferson got himself down from his father's shoulders and took off toward the dog pack. Austin started after him, doing some shouting of his own. His voice was lost in the screaming of a little brother, the horrendous howling of dogs—and the pounding of hoofbeats coming up behind.

Austin glanced over his shoulder in time to see a Ravenal horse thunder by, with a tawny-haired girl on its back. Grabbing his chest and gasping for air, Austin slowed to a stop and started to laugh.

Nobody could ride like that but Charlotte. Her horse split the pack, scattering bewildered hounds in every direction. The only one to emerge with his tail wagging was Bogie.

With a great splashing of mud, Charlotte made an about-face and galloped back around, Bogie flopping along behind her. She trotted to a halt and reached down a hand. Jefferson hauled himself up onto the horse's back. Together they passed Austin and reined in at Mother's side.

"Get on, Aunt Sally," Charlotte said.

"This is little shy Charlotte?" Father said.

"You've missed a great deal, Wesley," Mother said.

Charlotte waited until Mother and Jefferson were settled behind her and then stuck out her heels, ready to kick them in.

For the first time, Austin panicked. Charlotte never wanted anyone to see her cry, but not to say good-bye . . .

"Lottie!" he called.

Her legs stiffened out from the horse's sides, and for a moment it was as if everything were standing still. Even Jefferson was quiet.

"Remember," Austin said, "you promised to write to me!"

With her back still to him, she nodded.

"And I'll write back," he said. "And we'll see each other again. We will!"

She didn't nod this time. Instead, she slowly turned her head until her eyes rested on his face. They sparkled with tears.

She didn't have to say she believed him. He knew she did. He could tell from the way she lifted her chin and turned to crouch over the horse and dug in her heels. With Mother and Jefferson hanging on, she rode away—as if the faster she went, the sooner she would someday be back with Austin again.

"Where to, son?" his father said at his elbow.

"Kady's house," Austin said. But he didn't move until Charlotte was a speck in the distance.

"Lead the way, then," Father said.

Austin looked up at him. His great gray eyes were shining. Austin didn't ever remember seeing them that way before.

Although Austin picked the path, his father set a rapid pace. Austin took two steps to his one—but that didn't keep the questions from coming. Father explained as they went.

"There was nothing to do but come for you myself," he said. "Everyone told me, 'No, Wesley, you're a wanted man.' But how could I constantly risk my life to set slaves free and not even rescue my own family?"

"Risk your life?" Austin said. "What do you mean? Are you part of the Underground Railroad?"

"And proud of it," Father said. "I have stories to tell you, Austin. And I have a feeling you have a few of your own."

"You're part of the Underground Railroad?" Austin said again.

Father showed the faint trace of a smile. "Surprising for a weakling like myself, eh?"

Austin looked at him quickly—but Father was pointing ahead of them. "Is that where we're going?" he said.

And just like everything else that had happened since he'd gotten out of bed that morning, things picked up again and hurtled forward at breakneck speed.

Kady pulled them in the front door, glancing anxiously out behind them. Her face was grim.

"I sent Charlotte on with Bogie—the western direction," she said. "With Fitz gone taking Tot and Henry-James, I can't take any chances."

"Have we put you in a bad position?" Mother said.

"Aunt Sally, you set me free. I'm honored to do the same for you."

"What *about* Tot and Henry-James?" Austin asked. "They'll be all right, won't they?"

Kady's face went soft. "I'm as sure about that as I am of my own name," she said. "Fitz made special arrangements for them. They're going straight to Canada. *No one* can touch them there."

Austin's father looked at them all, his eyes serious. "I do have a great deal to catch up on," he said. "This may take the rest of our lives!"

"If you're going to *have* a rest of your life, we have to move quickly," Kady said. Her tone grew brisk again. "We have trunks to pack."

"We haven't brought any of our things," Mother said.

"I'm not talking about your things," Kady said.

Austin started to nod. "She's talking about us."

One by one, the Hutchinsons climbed into the trunks Kady had waiting in the back of her wagon—Mother in one, Father in another, Austin in still a third—

But Jefferson's face shriveled like a prune when Kady lifted him toward his.

"I'm afraid!" he cried. "I'm afraid to get in there!"

Austin looked at his own trunk, one big enough for him to actually lie down in.

"It's only until I can get you in the baggage car, Jefferson," Kady said. "One of our conductors will meet you in Richmond and then—"

"I'm afraid!"

"Jefferson," Austin said. "Why don't you come in with me?"

Kady looked at Austin doubtfully.

"It's all right," Austin said. "He's just a shrimp, after all."

"I am not either," Jefferson said. And he climbed into Austin's trunk.

"This is going to be a long trip to the baggage car," Kady whispered with a twinkle in her eye. "We have to go up to the next depot, where they aren't searching everyone's belongings. One of *our* conductors will be there."

"It's all right."

"You're a good man, Austin Hutchinson."

Austin ducked into the trunk without answering. No good-byes, Uncle Drayton had said. It was one of the few good ideas his uncle had ever had.

As soon as Kady had time to get up to her seat, the wagon lurched forward. Suddenly, that squirrel was back in Austin's throat.

They'd gotten away—from the Fire Eaters and the soldiers and the dogs—but it had all happened so fast. There had been no time to turn around just one more time and look.

He imagined the South Carolina that was passing them now—the palmettos he used to think looked like surprised hands, the snakes he'd never gotten to see hanging from the trees, the slaves in their cabins, believing that someday Jesus would set them free.

Suddenly, he wanted to throw open the lid and stretch his neck out and see it and hear it and smell it just one more time.

And tease Polly until she tossed her homely curls.

And read with Henry-James on a blanket by the rice fields.

And sit at Daddy Elias's feet and hear the Jesus stories.

And race down Slave Street with Charlotte—just one more time.

Who's going to be her friend now? he thought. *Polly? Bogie? Ria?*

That sounded like a wonderful group. He'd give a lot to have them with him, the way they were going to have each other.

What about me? Will I ever have friends again? Where's that feeling I had—when I knew I had to help Henry-James? When I knew just what to do?

"Austin?" Jefferson whispered.

"What?" Austin whispered back.

"Are you crying?"

"Yes," Austin said.

"I think I'm going to, too."

"You can."

"You won't think I'm a baby?"

"No, you aren't a baby."

"What am I, then?" Jefferson said.

Austin swallowed hard. "When you aren't screaming your head off or driving people into the insane asylum, you're . . . you're just who Jesus wants you to be."

"Does He like me?" Jefferson said. "I mean, you would know. You know Jesus as good as anybody—as good as Daddy Elias, even."

Austin couldn't answer him.

"Tell me a Jesus story," Jefferson said. "The way he used to. Then I won't be scared."

Austin swallowed again. From very close by, he heard a soft knock.

"Hello there," he heard his father say, his voice hollow in his trunk.

"We're here," Jefferson whispered loudly.

"How are you, men?" Father said.

"We men are fine, Father," Jefferson said.

Austin heard his father chuckle. Heard his mother giggle. Heard the wagon pulling them back toward the North, where a new life was about to begin.

And he could have sworn he heard Henry-James say, "You'll think of somethin', Massa Austin. You always do."

There's More Adventure in the CHRISTIAN HERITAGE SERIES!

The Salem Years, 1689–1691

The Rescue #1

Josiah Hutchinson's sister Hope is terribly ill. Can a stranger—whose presence could destroy the family's relationship with everyone else in Salem Village—save her?

The Stowaway #2

Josiah's dream of becoming a sailor seems within reach. But will the evil schemes of a tough orphan named Simon land Josiah and his sister in a heap of trouble?

The Guardian #3

Josiah has a plan to deal with the wolves threatening the town. Can he carry it out without endangering himself—or Cousin Rebecca, who'll follow him anywhere?

The Accused #4

Robbed by the cruel Putnam brothers, Josiah suddenly finds himself on trial for crimes he didn't commit. Can he convince anyone of his innocence?

The Samaritan #5

Josiah tries to help a starving widow and her daughter. But will his feud with the Putnams wreck everything he's worked for?

The Secret #6

If Papa finds out who Hope's been sneaking away to see, he'll be furious! Josiah knows her secret; should he tell?

The Williamsburg Years, 1780–1781

The Rebel #1

Josiah's great-grandson, Thomas Hutchinson, didn't rob the apothecary shop where he works. So why does he wind up in jail, and will he ever get out?

The Thief #2

Someone's stealing horses in Williamsburg! But is the masked rider Josiah sees the real culprit, and who's behind the mask?

The Burden #3

Thomas knows secrets he can't share. So what can he do when a crazed Walter Clark holds him at gunpoint over a secret he doesn't even know?

The Prisoner #4

As war rages in Williamsburg, Thomas' mentor refuses to fight and is carried off by the Patriots. Now which side will Thomas choose?

The Invasion #5

Word comes that Benedict Arnold and his men are ransacking plantations. Can Thomas and his family protect their homestead—even when it's invaded by British soldiers who take Caroline as a hostage?

The Battle #6

Thomas is surrounded by war! Can he tackle still another fight, taking orders from a woman he doesn't like—and being forbidden to talk about his missing brother?

The Charleston Years, 1860–1861

The Misfit #1

When the crusade to abolish slavery reaches full swing, Thomas Hutchinson's great-grandson Austin is sent to live with slave-holding relatives. How can he ever fit in?

The Ally #2

Austin resolves to teach young slave Henry-James to read, even though it's illegal. If Uncle Drayton finds out, will both boys pay the ultimate price?

The Threat #3

Trouble follows Austin to Uncle Drayton's vacation home. Who are those two men Austin hears scheming against his uncle—and why is a young man tampering with the family stagecoach?

The Trap #4

Austin's slave friend Henry-James beats hired hand Narvel in a wrestling match. Will Narvel get the revenge he seeks by picking fights and trapping Austin in a water well?

The Hostage #5

As north and south move toward civil war, Austin is kidnapped by men determined to stop his father from preaching against slavery. Can he escape?

The Escape #6

With the Civil War breaking out, Austin tries to keep Uncle Drayton from selling Henry-James at the slave auction. Will it work, and can Austin flee South Carolina with the rest of the Hutchinsons before Confederate soldiers find them?

The Chicago Years, 1928–1929

The Trick #1

Rudy and Hildy Helen Hutchinson and their father move to Chicago to live with their rich great-aunt Gussie. Can they survive the bullies they find—not to mention Little Al, a young schemer with hopes of becoming a mobster?

The Chase #2

Rudy and his family face one problem after another—including an accident that sends Rudy to the doctor, and the disappearance of Little Al. But can they make it through a deadly dispute between the mob and the Ku Klux Klan?

The Capture #3

It's Christmastime, but Rudy finds nothing to celebrate. Will his attorney father's defense of a Jewish boy accused of murder—and Hildy Helen's kidnapping—ruin far more than the holiday?

The Stunt #4

Rudy gets in trouble wing-walking on a plane. But can he stay standing as he finds himself in the middle of a battle for racial equality—and Aunt Gussie's dangerous fight for workers' rights?

Available at a Christian bookstore near you

FOCUS ON THE FAMILY®

Like this book?

Then you'll love *Clubhouse* magazine! It's written for kids just like you, and it's loaded with great stories, interesting articles, puzzles, games, and fun things for you to do. Some issues include posters, too! With your parents' permission, we'll even send you a complimentary copy.

Simply write to Focus on the Family, Colorado Springs, CO 80995 (in Canada, write P.O. 9800, Stn. Terminal, Vancouver, B.C. V6B 4G3) and mention that you saw this offer in the back of this book. Or, call 1-800-A-FAMILY (in Canada, call 1-800-661-9800).

You may also visit our Web site (www.family.org) to learn more about the ministry or find out if there is a Focus on the Family office in your country.

• • •

"Adventures in Odyssey" is a fantastic series of books, videos, and radio dramas that's fun for the entire family—parents, too! You'll love the twists and turns found in the novels, as well as the excitement packed into every video. And the 30 albums of radio dramas (available on audiocassette or compact disc) are great to listen to in the car, after dinner . . . even at bedtime! You can hear "Adventures in Odyssey" on the radio, too. Call Focus on the Family for a listing of local stations airing these programs or to request any of the "Adventures in Odyssey" resources. They're also available at Christian bookstores everywhere.

Focus on the Family is an organization that is dedicated to helping you and your family establish lasting, loving relationships with each other and the Lord. It's why we exist! If we can assist you or your family in any way, please feel free to contact us. We'd love to hear from you!